SPECIAL MESSAGE TO READERS

This book is published under the auspices of

THE ULVERSCROFT FOUNDATION

(registered charity No. 264873 UK)

Established in 1972 to provide funds for research, diagnosis and treatment of eye diseases. Examples of contributions made are: —

A Children's Assessment Unit at Moorfield's Hospital, London.

•

Twin operating theatres at the Western Ophthalmic Hospital, London.

•

A Chair of Ophthalmology at the Royal Australian College of Ophthalmologists.

•

The Ulverscroft Children's Eye Unit at the Great Ormond Street Hospital For Sick Children, London.

You can help further the work of the Foundation by making a donation or leaving a legacy. Every contribution, no matter how small, is received with gratitude. Please write for details to:

THE ULVERSCROFT FOUNDATION,
The Green, Bradgate Road, Anstey,
Leicester LE7 7FU, England.
Telephone: (0116) 236 4325

In Australia write to:

THE ULVERSCROFT FOUNDATION,
c/o The Royal Australian and New Zealand
College of Ophthalmologists,
94-98 Chalmers Street, Surry Hills,
N.S.W. 2010, Australia

THE TURNING TIDE

Eleanor Faversham's only contact with London's society is through her employment in her uncle's shoe shop — but when she decides to attend the local Assembly Rooms in the guise of a French émigrée, she meets the dashing Lord Stansfield. Betrayed by a jealous cousin, Eleanor is banished from her home and flung onto the streets of London. A further chance encounter with Lord Stansfield leads her into a world of intrigue and danger — and her life will never be the same again!

Books by Karen Abbott
in the Linford Romance Library:

RED ROSE GIRL
SUMMER ISLAND
A TIME TO FORGIVE
LOVE IS BLIND
LOVE CONQUERS ALL
A MATTER OF TRUST
DESIGNS FOR LOVE
WHEN TRUE LOVE WINS
A TASTE OF HAPPINESS
THE HEART KNOWS NO BOUNDS

KAREN ABBOTT

THE TURNING TIDE

Complete and Unabridged

LINFORD
Leicester

First published in Great Britain in 2003

First Linford Edition
published 2004

British Library CIP Data

Abbott, Karen
The turning tide.—Large print ed.—
Linford romance library
1. Love stories
2. Large type books
I. Title
823.9′14 [F]

ISBN 1–84395–360–9

Published by
F. A. Thorpe (Publishing)
Anstey, Leicestershire

Set by Words & Graphics Ltd.
Anstey, Leicestershire
Printed and bound in Great Britain by
T. J. International Ltd., Padstow, Cornwall

This book is printed on acid-free paper

1

Eleanor Faversham gazed dreamily out of the window of her uncle's shoe shop, wishing with all the might of her twenty-one years that she could be outside in the brilliant sunshine instead of here in this stuffy room.

It was 1793 and King George the Third reigned on the throne of England. London wasn't the best place to be in late summer. The worst of the heat was over and many of the ton were returning to their town houses, but it was still uncomfortably warm and the interior of the shop was airless.

Footwear of many styles, sizes and colours competed for the attention of wealthy customers. The gentlemen, from titled lords and ladies, to the more humble men of commerce, were ushered through an archway into Gerard Faversham's own domain, where he measured and fitted for bespoke items or passed the customers on to Abel Jenkins, his senior apprentice, to select and fit the ready-to-wear.

The ladies came to the left-hand side, where Eleanor would greet them, offer them a seat, measure their feet, ask their requirements and help them to make their selection of ready-to-wear or bespoke shoes, slippers and boots. Gerard Faversham had been known to keep his cobblers at work throughout the night to complete a speciality of ready-to-wear or bespoke shoes, slippers and boots. The quality and variety of the footwear in the shop attracted customers from throughout London and the Home Counties.

Gerard Faversham was doing very nicely, especially since his niece saved him from the inconvenience of having to employ someone to assist him in the ladies' department. That would eat into his profit somewhat.

A grand carriage had drawn up at the front of the shop. A fashionably-dressed woman descended from it, her silken gown trailing the ground behind her. Turning from the window, Eleanor sighed as she glanced down at her own humble gown. Her attire was plain and hard-wearing, the colour dark and serviceable. How she would love to dress in lighter colours and feel the softness of silk and satin on her skin!

'Eleanor! Stop daydreaming, girl! We have a new customer. Attend to Mistress Dudley at once! Do you hear?'

'Yes, Uncle,' she murmured dutifully, moving away from the window.

He turned to smile ingratiatingly at the haughty-looking woman who tapped her foot impatiently on the ground as she waited.

'My niece is at your complete service, Mistress Dudley. A drink of cordial, perhaps, whilst you wait?' he said.

'I have no intention of waiting, my good man! Your emporium was recommended to me as being of the highest quality but if I am not attended to immediately, I shall take my custom elsewhere!'

She raised her lorgnette and glared disdainfully through it as Eleanor hurried towards her.

'I'm with you, right now, mistress,' Eleanor said hastily, drawing up a straight-backed chair for her client. 'Please be seated whilst I take down your requirements. Maybe your maid would like to go through to the back to choose some refreshment for you, Mistress Dudley?'

She smiled sideways at the young woman of about her own age.

'Do tell my cousin, Charlotte, what your mistress requires. You may prefer to stay with her until your mistress is ready to depart,' Eleanor added.

The young woman gave her a grateful smile and hurried away in the direction Eleanor indicated. Mistress Dudley removed her long gloves as she inclined her head in acknowledgement of Eleanor's service.

Shortly afterwards, Eleanor's cousin,

Charlotte, glided into the shop, carrying a small tray on which sat a jug of cordial and a crystal-cut glass. Her lips were pressed together tightly, Eleanor noticed, hiding a tiny smile. Charlotte held too high an opinion of herself to enjoy serving the customers in her father's shop. Her pale eyes glimmered with suppressed annoyance as she caught Eleanor's satisfied grin. She placed the tray on a small table at the side of their client, bobbed the briefest of curtsies and glided back to the rear portion of the establishment, her back rigid.

Eleanor pulled a wry face as her cousin disappeared, knowing that she would hear more about it later! She pursed her lips. Because Charlotte was Gerard's daughter and faintly laid claim to a weakness of health, she didn't have to work in the shop, a duty that had been laid upon Eleanor since she had been old enough to help her uncle carry the heavy skins of leather and sweep up the cuttings from the floor at the end of the long days.

Eleanor sighed restlessly. Surely there was more to life than these seemingly endless days of measuring feet and stitching intricate designs into pieces of leather. And all the while, Charlotte sat at ease, painting or stitching small samplers, her pale hands as smooth as silk. At nineteen, Charlotte was well capable of helping Eleanor or rather would have been so, if she had ever been made to try.

Pushing away her resentful thoughts, Eleanor listened attentively to Mistress Dudley's list of requirements and directed her thoughts to some new skins of the softest kid that had recently been acquired and swiftly sketched a new design that would make her new shoes a joy to behold.

'Exactly the idea I had in the first place, dear,' Mistress Dudley now amiably agreed, with the satisfied smile on her much-powdered face, already imagining herself in her newly-made shoes. 'Now, I have here a pair of slippers that need to be resoled. I need them this very evening. I am told that Mr Faversham conducts a speedy business!' she added sharply, her eyebrows rising a fraction. 'I trust that doesn't present a problem.'

'No, no, of course not,' Eleanor hastened to assure her. 'My uncle will see to them at once, I am sure, and we will deliver them to you as soon as they are ready. May I take down your address?'

Mistress Dudley rose to her feet.

'You may gather my details from Rivers, my dear. I have a busy time ahead of me and I cannot delay any further. Tell Rivers to follow me on foot. I bid you good day.'

She swept from the shop across the narrow pavement to her carriage. Eleanor took the pair of satin slippers to her uncle, explaining Mistress Dudley's demand, hoping he wouldn't be cross at her for agreeing to it. Fortunately, he wasn't. He nodded in agreement.

'Anything to secure a new customer.

Did you get her details?'

'I'm just about to do so, Uncle. Mistress Dudley's maid is in the back. I'll do it quickly whilst we have no other customers.'

She was glad of the short break and took the opportunity to pour herself a glass of cordial to refresh her thirst. The maid, Rivers, wasn't surprised at being abandoned by her mistress.

'Have you far to go?' Eleanor asked her anxiously.

'Nay! About half a mile,' Rivers reckoned. 'It's partway down Golders Lane. You know, where the Assembly Rooms are?'

'Really? You live near the Assembly Rooms?'

'Right in them!'

The maid, who had introduced herself as Sally, laughed.

'At least, I live in the attic. Mistress Dudley runs the place!'

'Oh, do tell me what it's like!'

Eleanor clasped her hands together in front of her in anticipation of the delights she knew she would hear.

'The rooms are lovely! All bright with softly-covered walls and shining lights, and lots of flowers. And, oh, the rich peoples' clothes! It's how I think the King's palace must be like!'

Sally's voice held a touch of wonder.

'Oh, I'd love to see it,' Eleanor said wistfully.

It was a whole world away from her life in the shop. She closed her eyes and tried to imagine what it must be like, but she couldn't.

'Oh, I'd be satisfied for ever if I could just have a peep at it!'

A sudden idea made her gasp at its daring and her eyes gleamed with anticipation. She glanced where her cousin was sitting in a rocking chair, idly rocking back and forth, stroking the cat, asleep on her lap, then looked back at Sally. She kept her voice low.

'Is there an Assembly tonight?'

Sally nodded.

'Why do you enquire?'

With a gasp of excitement, Eleanor

took hold of Sally's hands.

'I'd love to see it! What do you think? Do you think I may?'

Sally's look of bewilderment gave way to the dawning of understanding.

'When? Tonight?'

Eleanor nodded.

'Why not? I'll get my uncle to allow me to bring Mistress Dudley's slippers and I could slip in somewhere to see the finery! Oh, I've longed to be able to do so. It would only take a minute. Nobody will even notice.'

Sally considered for a moment, then a slow smile spread across her face.

'I suppose I shouldn't, really, but why not!'

Throughout the remainder of the afternoon there was a steady stream of customers and Eleanor had no time for further dreaming.

'Uncle, I wish you would instruct Charlotte to help me to serve the customers,' she grumbled at the end of the afternoon.

Her face was red from the heat and

exertion, whereas Charlotte, curled up in an easy chair, looked neat and cool.

'It isn't fair! I'm exhausted! You ought to help, Charlotte!'

'Now, you know your cousin is delicate,' Gerard reproved her. 'She's like her dear mamma and mustn't exert herself in this heat.'

His wife had passed away five years earlier, as much worn out by her hard work as from her frailty of health, Eleanor considered. Certainly, Charlotte was in no danger of doing likewise! Charlotte flashed her a smug smile, and Eleanor glared back.

'Why, Eleanor! You know my fingers get sore with chilblains in the winter and my chest hurts!' Charlotte quietly protested, her eyes large and innocent. 'And I feel so weak in the present heat!'

Her hand fluttered towards her throat.

'I can't breathe properly! How can you be so cruel, Eleanor? You don't know what it is like to suffer so.'

Charlotte looked so pained that Eleanor

regretted her outburst instantly.

'I'm sorry, dearest. You're right!' Eleanor said wryly. 'I'm too healthy for my own good. Just look at me!'

She was of average height and her body slim. Her hair was dark and her skin, though fair, had a healthy glow to it, unlike Charlotte, who, without doubt, was thin and pale.

'I didn't mean to upset you, Charlotte, dear. It's just that it has been so hot in there today. I have only to tidy the shop and we can have our meal. Do you know if Tabby needs help in preparing it?'

Tabitha, their only servant, heard her voice and came shuffling out of the small kitchen that led off from the side of the room they were in. She had been with them for many years, originally as Charlotte's nurse. Without her help and loyalty, Eleanor knew her uncle would never have succeeded in continuing his business. Tabitha gave her a smile of acknowledgment.

'Don't you be worrying about that,

Miss Eleanor. Them as should be worrying don't!'

With a sideways jerk of her head towards Charlotte, she turned back into the kitchen. Eleanor made a wry grimace as she returned to the shop. She tidied it swiftly, swept the floor and dusted the counters. Her uncle entered, Mistress Dudley's slippers in his hand.

'Leave it for now, Eleanor. It's time to eat,' he said. 'Then you can take these slippers round to Mistress Dudley. Ask her if she wishes to open an account. Our wealthier customers seem to find it more agreeable to do so.'

Eleanor smiled. For all his gruff ways with her in the shop, he appreciated all her work, she was sure, though he didn't often say so.

After they had eaten, Eleanor turned to Charlotte.

'Charlotte, why don't you come, with me? It will do you good, I'm sure.'

Charlotte's pretty face pouted at once.

'In faith, Eleanor, you have the

strangest of ideas. Of course it won't do me good. Tell her, Father. The exertion would be far too much for me.'

Gerard, who had seated himself at his high desk and was doing the day's accounts, looked up sharply from his papers.

'Pray, stop this quarrelling. How am I to complete the accounts if you two are caterwauling like a pair of fishwives in Billingsgate market?'

'But I need a companion, Uncle! I cannot go on my own,' Eleanor pointed out. 'There may be footpads about.'

'Take Tabitha. She can finish her work later.'

With no more ado, he bent his head over his columns of figures and resumed his calculations.

As Eleanor and Tabitha traversed the streets, Eleanor felt a wild excitement burning within her. She was familiar with the up-to-date fashions of every-day wear of the upper-classes, but she had never seen any of the sumptuous dresses of the court and high society. It was going to be a wonderful spectacle! She could hardly contain herself as they approached a large, ornate building that was set back from the road.

Horse-drawn carriages were already drawing up outside the magnificent flight of steps that led up to the front entrance, ablaze with light. Pulling herself away from the intoxicating scene, Eleanor led the way down the side of the building and found the rear entrance. She could hear sounds of pans being scraped and appetising smells drifted through the doorway to what must surely be the kitchen. Her whole body sizzled with excitement as she awaited an answer to her rapping at the door. The door was pulled open and a young servant appeared in front of her.

'What d'you want?' she asked truculently, then seeing the package still tucked under Eleanor's arm, she held out her hand. 'Give it here, then.'

Eleanor hugged the package to her chest.

'It's a personal delivery, for Mistress Dudley. May I come in? Mistress

Dudley is expecting me.'

The girl opened the door wider.

'Well, I suppose you'd best come in then. D'you know your way up? I haven't got time to take you. We're mad busy tonight!'

'Yes, so I see. I'm sure I'll find my way. I can always ask someone, can't I?' Eleanor replied airily, trusting she could find her way. 'You wait here, Tabitha. Your poor legs won't make it up all the stairs.'

Tabitha looked relieved to be going no farther and she shuffled into the kitchen, whilst Eleanor ran up the stairs, her heart thudding. At the first landing, the uncarpeted passage divided into two. Now, which way? There was a door to the right and she pushed it open tentatively. Holding her breath, she stepped through the doorway. She was in a long, oak-panelled gallery. A rich red carpet ran down the centre of the gallery, with highly-polished floorboards at its edge. She had never seen anything so grand!

Large paintings hung on the wall. Some were portraits of distinguished-looking personages, others were landscapes and seascapes.

A door farther along the passage opened and Eleanor jumped. It was Sally. With a sigh of relief, Eleanor ran towards her.

'Sally! Oh, I'm glad it's you! I've brought the repaired slippers to your mistress but the servant downstairs didn't have time to bring me up.'

'Come with me. Mistress Dudley is in her boudoir. That means her bedroom. We use a lot of fancy words here.'

Eleanor followed Sally along the carpeted floor, drinking in the wonder of everything they passed.

'It's so beautiful,' she murmured, filled with awe.

She realised that Sally had stopped and was holding open a door. Craning her neck to peer inside, Eleanor gasped again. The room was light and airy, totally unlike their own living quarters behind and above the shop. Large windows ran along the whole of one side of the room, with long golden drapes that reached from the ceiling to the floor, topped by valances made of swathes of the same material. Dusky pink wall coverings, with yet more paintings hanging upon them, were the backdrop to the elegant furniture that was tastefully arranged around the room.

'Ah, Rivers! There you are!'

Mistress Dudley swept into the room dressed in a much-frilled day-gown, her immaculate, bouffant hair framing her well-powdered face.

'And who is this?'

Eleanor dropped a short curtsey.

'Mistress Dudley,' she murmured, 'my uncle has sent me to return your slippers. I hope you haven't been kept waiting for them.'

'Ah, yes! Master Faversham's niece. They are repaired?'

'Yes, mistress. May I try them on your feet to make sure they fit comfortably? My uncle used the softest of leather on the soles. I'm sure you will find them delightful to dance in.'

'Heavens, dear! I don't do much dancing!'

Her light laughter brought a faint blush to Eleanor's cheeks.

'But, I am on my feet all evening, so it is important that my feet are comfortable!' she added, noticing Eleanor's discomfort. 'They are perfect!'

She smiled in satisfaction at her extended foot.

'I think I am going to enjoy dealing with your uncle. Will you ask him to set up an account for me, dear?'

Upon Eleanor's agreement, Mistress Dudley excused herself.

'My guests are already arriving and I must descend to greet them. Rivers will show you out.'

Sally waited until her mistress had swept from the room.

'Come on. We'll have to be quick. I'll show you where to go but I won't be able to stay with you. You'll know your way out again, won't you? All the back stairs lead down to the kitchen eventually. Don't let anyone catch sight of you or I'll be for it!'

Eleanor followed Sally back along the corridor, her heart thudding wildly with excitement. As they reached a door set into the panel work, Sally put a finger across her lips and touched Eleanor's arm.

'It's through here. It's the servants' door to the balcony,' she whispered. 'It won't be busy tonight but keep your ears skinned. Couples sometimes slip up here for a bit of kissing and cuddling! I'll get back to you if I can.'

When Sally had slipped away, Eleanor cautiously opened the door. The huge room beyond was glittering with light and colour. She held her breath as she tiptoed forward to the edge of the balcony. She was at its extreme right-hand side where a dark red velvet curtain hung from the high ceiling to the balcony floor. She melted into its folds and gazed in awed wonder.

Her main impression was of mid

blue, silver and gold, with sparkling patterns cast by the glittering chandeliers and the heady scent of a multitude of enclosed flowers. It was all Sally had promised, and more! She looked downwards, past the elaborate garlands of exotic plants, into the crowded ballroom of silks, satins and brocades. It was a kaleidoscope of colour and took her breath away. Her lips parted in delight as she looked down.

The delicate strains of a minuet floated into the air, merging with the buzz of talk and laughter. Eleanor watched entranced as the couples formed their sets and began the intricate steps and patterns of the dance. She watched wide-eyed at the long-legged, pointed toes of the gentlemen, their hands held delicately aloft, fingers entwined with the ladies, who were perfectly balanced in their swaying gowns, turning this way and that.

Eleanor was enchanted. She had to become part of this glittering world! But, how was she to do it? The musical sound of a woman's laughter caught her attention and sent her sliding back into the folds of the curtain. The laughter was drawing nearer, followed by the lower tones of a male voice.

'Lord Stansfield, I declare you are teasing me!'

'Tease you, my dear Lavinia? Never!'

Eleanor risked peeping out from the folds. She saw the woman called Lavinia tap the man's arm with her folded fan.

'You are the world's greatest flirt! Remember, I am a married lady!'

'Fie, Lavinia! Since when did marriage stop a renowned rake such as I?'

He leaned towards his companion and whispered something in her ear. Eleanor couldn't see his face as his back was towards her. His hair was dark, unpowdered and cut short into his neck, as the fashion was now dictating. He was tall and well-proportioned, and obviously of little moral character, she thought disapprovingly.

The man's voice had lost its bantering tone when he spoke again.

'But, enough of these pleasantries, Lavinia. What news have you?'

'La, sir! You are too impatient! A little dalliance goes not amiss! Eyes may be upon us. You must make more court of me!'

Eleanor peeped out again, in time to see the gentleman make an elaborate bow, sweeping his hand out to the side as if he were flourishing a hat. Frills of cream lace dangled at the wrists of his long-sleeved, pale green satin suit. His pantaloons were a perfect fit to his well-shaped legs. Eleanor felt a stir of interest arise deep within her. It was a new experience to be so close to a well-appointed man. Although many ladies and their maids tripped over the threshold of their shop, it was usually only the more elderly of husbands who chose to accompany their wives on such errands.

She watched as the man held the lady's hand and kissed the tips of her fingers, murmuring, 'At your service, madam!'

Lavinia's musical laugh rippled forth once more.

'Very well, Jeremy. Any spies must now be convinced that you have led me here solely to rob me of my virtue! Therefore I will pass on the message from my brother. A consignment of, shall we say, precious cargo will be ready for despatch from Calais two nights hence on the evening tide. He trusts that you will be ready to ship the goods across the Channel and that you have arranged for them to disappear for a while.'

Eleanor's hand flew to her mouth, her eyes wide with a mixture of consternation and excitement. The man must be a smuggler! The consignments wine and brandy! How thrilling! Lavinia appeared not to share the thrill, only the awareness of his possible danger.

'You will take care, Jeremy, dear? You know how distraught I would be if ought should befall you!' she urged in low tones.

She snapped her fan closed and

tapped Jeremy's arm again.

'I think it is time you returned me to my husband.'

She turned as she spoke, drawing Lord Stansfield with her. Her voice faded, and Eleanor waited a few moments, anxious to make her escape.

She was about to let the folds of the curtains fall when a hand grasped hold of her shoulder and pulled her backwards.

2

Eleanor screamed as a hand was placed swiftly over her mouth. Completely unnerved, she tried to fight her way free but was held far too securely.

'If you stop struggling and promise not to scream, I will release you,' a male voice hissed in her ear.

Recognising that she had no other option, Eleanor forced herself to relax and grunted her assent through the firm fingers across her mouth. The hold on her relaxed and turned her round. She found herself facing the now dark and threatening face of the courtly gentleman who had been conversing with the Lady Lavinia. Eleanor's previous joy of the occasion evaporated into the heavily-scented air. She felt a stab of fear. A strange weakness in her knees made her fear that she might be about to faint.

'Why were you hiding behind the curtain?' he asked sharply. 'Were you spying on your betters?'

'No,' Eleanor stammered. 'That is, I only wished to watch the dancing. I had no intention of eavesdropping. I am sorry, my lord.'

She dropped her eyes into what she hoped was a demure gesture, automatically using the title that she had heard Lady Lavinia use. Strangely, as she spoke, she was no longer afraid. There was an aura of strength about this man, as much comforting as intimidating, and she had done nothing wrong, had she? Not really wrong, she amended to herself.

'But eavesdrop you did! Tell me, what did you hear? I will know if you lie!'

She felt her eyes drawn to his and was startled by the intensity of their blueness. They were as cold as steel and seemed to penetrate into her soul.

'I didn't really hear anything, my lord. Only something of . . . was it Calais? But I'm not sure what that means. Is it foreign?'

The man's eyes studied her face, searching, she was sure, for some sign of duplicity. He seemed satisfied.

'Yes, it is foreign,' he replied briefly, 'but it is of no consequence. You needn't trouble your pretty little head about it.'

He paused, the thumb and first finger of his right hand stroking his chin.

'Who are you?' he asked suddenly. 'Why are you here?'

Eleanor thought quickly.

'I'm . . . er . . . Ella,' she said, using the diminutive form of her name, casting down her eyes again. 'I'm new here, my lord.'

With any luck, he might think her a simple servant girl.

'I just wanted to see the finery. I've never seen the like of it.'

The man stepped back a little, his eyes still narrowed and distrustful. He regarded her silently and Eleanor felt she observed some of the tension leave his face.

'I only intended to stay for a moment or two, my lord. I was alarmed when I heard you approaching. I shouldn't really be here.'

She was glad that most of her hair was hidden beneath the cotton cap she wore, and, surely, one servant looked just like another to the nobility. She bobbed a curtsey.

'Mistress Dudley will be wondering where I am, my lord. There is much work to be done for our guests, you realise.'

The mention of Mistress Dudley seemed to allay his suspicions of her.

'Then, take heed! Mistress Dudley is well-known to me. She will not be pleased if I tell of your intrusion here.'

'No, my lord, though I meant no harm. May I depart now?'

She began to edge her way past him, towards the inner doorway. Dreading that he was about to detain her further, she made a rush for the door and whirled through it. She leaned against the wall for a moment, to compose her features. She still had to get out of here undetected, if possible. She hurried along the passageway and down the stairs, unsure of how long she had been on the balcony. To her relief, Tabitha, her face anxious, was just emerging from the kitchen.

'There you be, Miss Eleanor. Wherever have you been? I thought you had got quite lost up there.'

'No, no, Tabitha. I . . . er . . . took just a peek at the dancing. It was lovely, but we must be leaving.'

She was suddenly anxious to be gone in case the man had reported her presence. She hoped not. She would never forgive herself if Sally got into trouble for her complicity in the small adventure.

Over the next few days, Eleanor's head was in a whirl of excitement and fanciful dreams. The unfortunate encounter at the end of her escapade pushed to the back of her mind, she would float around the shop in rhythm to the tunes that were swirling around in her head.

'Keep your mind on your work, Eleanor!' Gerard snapped more than once. 'And cease from this prancing around the floor. If this is what your small brush with Society brings, maybe I'd better send Charlotte next time!'

Eleanor held her breath. Charlotte had absolutely no interest in her father's business and no rapport with their customers.

'Oh, don't do that, Uncle Gerard! I only had a little peek over the balcony at the dancing when I was there the other night, and it was just wonderful!'

'Don't you be getting ideas above your station!' Gerard warned, shaking his head. 'You are too like your mamma, God rest her soul, always dreaming flights of fancy, talking of the nobility as though she were part of it, forever touching the satin slippers and such. Said they reminded her of her childhood days, foolish woman!'

'No, Uncle! She wasn't foolish! She was a lady! She told me!'

Unconsciously, she fingered the locket

at her neck, hidden beneath the material of her frock. It was the only memento of her mother. She believed it to hold her likeness, though she had never seen it, since the damaged clasp would not open.

'She used to tell me about the balls she went to.'

'Fiddle-faddle, Eleanor! Your mamma lived with her mind in the skies, especially after the death of my brother. She was no more than a lady's maid, as I have told you many times before!'

She lifted her face and looked intently at him.

'Uncle Gerard, I know you mean well but I am sure Mamma spoke the truth. She wouldn't lie to me. She wouldn't!'

Her face saddened as her fingers caressed the smooth golden locket that bore an engraved crest.

'She said she would tell me everything when I was twenty-one, but she was long dead by then.'

'Nonsense, girl! Your mamma was a weak, foolish woman whose mind went after my brother's death! Now, no more of this nonsense!'

The jangling of the bell above the main door brought a welcome diversion. A well-dressed manservant entered the shop, holding out a letter.

'For Master Faversham,' he declared.

Gerard strode forward and took it from the man's hand. He read it quickly, looking sharply towards Eleanor.

'Eleanor!' he exclaimed.

'Yes, Uncle?'

'This letter is from Mistress Dudley. She says . . . '

Eleanor felt a hot flush spread over her face. Her hand fluttered at her throat. Oh, dear! Had her escapade at the ball been discovered?

'I'm sorry, Uncle. I . . . '

'Sorry? Don't be sorry, girl! It's wonderful news! She is very impressed with you, Eleanor. She has recommended you to a friend of hers, a member of the nobility, no less! She wants you to take a supply of shoes and slippers suitable for a young lady of fashion to Lady Harrington this afternoon at Harrington Mansion. Just think of it, Eleanor, the nobility!'

Gerard turned to address the messenger.

'Tell your mistress that my niece will do as she has been asked.'

He dropped the letter on to the counter top, rubbing his hands together.

'This could be the start of a new enterprise! There is no better recommendation than that of a satisfied customer! Come, read the letter! You must start to make your selection at once. There is no time to lose!'

'But where shall I start? How will I take them there?'

Eleanor's mind was whirling as she read the letter, but Gerard lifted his hands in the air in exasperation.

'Start anywhere! Select what you like. She will send her carriage! See! There, at the end!'

He paced up and down in excitement, pulling dainty, satin slippers and soft kid boots from their places.

'Here! Take these, and these! You

know what young ladies like! Oh, I've dreamed of this day! My name will be renowned.'

Eleanor set to with a will and quickly assembled together as many different styles as she thought might be suitable for the task, adding many of her own drawings of new styles not yet put into production. She felt her own excitement growing as she scurried about the showroom. If she pleased Lady Harrington, she might be invited to make a return visit and even be recommended to yet more customers. Oh, how exciting! But Charlotte was not pleased!

'I'm the daughter of the business!' she protested. 'It should be me who is going, not her!'

Eleanor paused from her activity.

'But you don't know anything about the making of shoes, Charlotte! You wouldn't know what to advise!'

'You could tell me!'

'Nonsense! Nonsense!' Gerard interrupted, siding with Eleanor for once. 'Besides, Lady Harrington has asked personally for Eleanor. No, you must remain here, Charlotte. It will be a good experience for you to be handling our customers where I am on hand to advise you. That is how they will come to know you. Before long, they will be asking for you by name also!'

'But it's not fair!' she pouted. 'Why should Eleanor get out of all the work? I will be quite exhausted before the day is done. You've done this on purpose, haven't you, Eleanor?'

'Silence, girl! Gerard admonished. 'Eleanor will be working as well.'

'But, Father!' Charlotte wailed.

Gerard opened his arms to embrace his daughter.

'Maybe another time, Charlotte, another time. Yes, Eleanor shall teach you, my dear.'

He then brushed her aside impatiently.

'But today it must be Eleanor who goes to Harrington Mansion.'

The carriage arrived at two o'clock. The coachman and Gerard loaded the packages that Eleanor had made ready and she climbed eagerly up into the well-upholstered carriage.

It was her very first ride in a carriage. She felt so grand. She pushed aside her nerves in the flurry of the excitement she felt as she bowled along the London streets to Harrington Mansion. She had never been this far from her home. Her eyes opened wide at the vast green spaces, the lakes, the ducks, the flower beds, the magnificent houses. She had thought London consisted of narrow streets and high town houses. This was beautiful!

All too soon, it seemed, the carriage slowed and turned in through some tall, wrought-iron gates set within an ivy-covered stone wall and turned into a cobbled courtyard at the rear of the building, where, eventually, Eleanor was handed down. She gazed around in interest. Even this rear aspect was far grander than anything she had ever seen, apart from the Assembly Rooms, that was. Her eyes danced with delight.

It was at least four storeys high, probably more, she decided, as she took a step backwards and gazed upwards. There were tiny windows set into the roof and yet more that descended below ground level at her feet, protected by a metal grill, the kitchen, no doubt, if the appetising aroma was anything to go by. But, enough of that! She was too excited at the prospect of going into the house to be over enthralled by its exterior.

'I'll get someone to take ye upstairs, miss,' the coachman assured her. 'Leave the packages. They'll be sent up.'

'I'll just take these,' Eleanor insisted, picking up a couple of the packages. 'Right! Lead on!'

A young kitchen maid led her as far as the dividing door between the front and back of the house, then a smartly-dressed parlour maid led her up the fine staircase. All was white paintwork adorned with gilt-framed pictures and mirrors. Chandeliers glittered in the sunlight streaming through the windows. The maid knocked gently on a double door, which she then opened and ushered Eleanor inside.

She paused on the threshold, gazing around in awe. It was a large, light and airy room with tall, arched windows. The paintwork was a very pale cream with wall coverings in vertical stripes of cream and gold. All the pictures and mirrors were framed in gold.

A gentle cough behind her made her realise that the maid was holding out her hands, indicating that Eleanor take off her cloak and bonnet. She undid the ties and slipped out of her outer clothing, still turning slowly round to take in all of the room. The golden carpet was deep and soft. Elegant furniture was tastefully arranged, the seats in matching gold and cream brocades. Gilt-framed, oval-backed chairs with curved legs stood alongside delicate-looking tables.

Another double door at the far end of the room opened and an elegantly-dressed woman of middle years entered the room. She was accompanied by a pretty, young lady, dressed in a gown that was at least two sizes too large for her. Eleanor was aware of the maid at her side curtseying low. Instinctively, Eleanor copied her. It was obviously the correct thing to do, for the woman smiled at her, indicating with her hand that she should rise.

'That will be all, Anna,' Lady Harrington said, her voice low and gentle. 'And you must be Eleanor Faversham.'

Her smile put Eleanor at her ease instantly.

'Yes, milady.'

She paused shyly, as Lady Harrington turned to draw the young woman forward.

'This is my . . . er . . . ward, Eleanor, Mademoiselle Adèle Aubrier.'

Eleanor dropped into a small curtsey. In spite of the girl's outsize clothing, she had an air of elegance about her that bespoke of some degree of nobility. The girl smiled shyly as she inclined her head.

'Enchantée, mademoiselle.'

Her voice was soft and musical.

'Mademoiselle Adèle is recently come from France, an émigrée,' Lady Harrington added softly. 'She needs a complete wardrobe, I'm afraid, poor child, and a complete set of new footwear. I am telling you this so that you may understand why we have asked you to come here, Eleanor. We don't want her circumstances to be generally known, as there could be danger for her, so I must ask you to be very discreet.'

Eleanor nodded, surprised at Lady Harrington's caution. Who would wish to harm this lovely creature?

'I have made a list of possible occasions to cater for,' Lady Harrington continued. 'You will find them on the small table over there. Once Mademoiselle Aubrier is clothed correctly, I will introduce her into Society, and, of course, the expense is of no consequence!'

A knock at the door interrupted their

conversation and a maid announced the arrival of the packages Eleanor had brought with her. Eleanor smiled at the young French lady, unsure how to address her.

'If you will come this way, mistress,' she invited the girl. 'I'm sure you will find plenty to please you.'

Adèle hesitated and cast a worried look at Lady Harrington. Lady Harrington inclined her head towards Eleanor.

'Mademoiselle Aubrier doesn't speak much English, I'm afraid.'

She turned back to the young lady and spoke some words quietly that Eleanor didn't understand.

'Ah, oui, madame. Yes, pleeze.'

Adèle smiled at Eleanor and followed her across the room. She was very pretty. Her dark brown hair was fashioned into ringlets gathered together and fastened to the left-hand side of her head, with just a few smaller ringlets framing her face. She fingered a white satin slipper with pale pink roses embroidered along its length.

‘Eeze nice, yes?’

Eleanor noticed that, although her eyes lit up when she spoke, a sadness lurked in her expression. She wondered what had caused it, but felt it would be unmannered to ask, even if Adèle knew enough English to tell her.

Eleanor smiled encouragingly.

‘Yes, they are very nice, mam’selle.’

‘You say, Adèle, yes?’

Eleanor glanced hesitantly at Lady Harrington. She nodded her agreement. Eleanor smiled at Adèle.

‘Yes, Adèle. Now, let me measure your feet and I will see if there is anything I’ve brought that will fit you.’

She laughed self-consciously, realising that Adèle wouldn’t have understood a word of what she had said. Nonetheless, without being able to understand each other fully, they were soon laughing and giggling and feeling as though they had known each other for ages. After finding a few pairs of shoes and slippers that fitted Adèle’s small feet, Eleanor selected some of the pieces of soft kid she had brought with her and showed Adèle some of her drawings, guiding her choices towards suitable styles.

Adèle showed her delight and Eleanor discovered that language was no barrier when the people concerned liked each other and were prepared to find other ways of communicating. She had taken to Adèle instantly and looked forward to getting to know her better. She might even be able to teach her a bit of English, though how she would do that without knowing any French, she wasn't sure. Lady Harrington smiled to see them.

'This is a lovely house,' Eleanor said at one point, glancing around at the room. 'Was your home like this?'

'Pardon, Eleanor? I not always comprend.'

Eleanor pointed to her.

'You, in France, like this?' she said, sweeping her arms round the room.

Adèle's face became sad.

'Ah, yes, my 'ome . . . eet ees très belle. But I go zaire no more.'

Eleanor sympathised with her sadness. It must be dreadful to have to leave your home and country and lose all that you held dear at one fell swoop. She had heard terrible tales of the recent events in France but couldn't imagine this lovely young lady having been caught up in them.

For the next couple of hours, Eleanor made notes and drawings, writing down various suggestions as to how her uncle could vary the designs of the shoes and boots Adèle liked. A maid brought in a tray of glasses of cordial and biscuits, all of which were perfectly delicious. The two young women sat on the floor amongst the scraps of kid and fabrics. It would be a gargantuan order. Her uncle was going to be well-pleased!

'For now, milady, I am finished. My uncle will begin the work tomorrow and I will return for fittings whenever necessary,' she said eventually.

'That will be perfectly in order, Eleanor, but, for today, I must ask Adèle to come upstairs now to be dressed. Lord Stansfield is dining with us tonight, Adèle. I am sure you will be pleased to meet with him once more.'

Eleanor was interested to notice that Adèle blushed prettily. So, she had caught the eye of the dashing Lord Stansfield, had she? She hoped he wasn't as libertine in character as his assignation with Lady Lavinia suggested he might be!

3

Eleanor hardly stopped dreaming wonderful fantasies over the next few days. She made a few extra visits to try her basic shoe design against Adèle's foot and made the few minor alterations that were necessary.

However, when requests for Eleanor to visit other customers in their homes began to trickle in, Gerard wasn't as pleased as Eleanor expected.

'I need you here,' he stated. 'Charlotte has found your absences far too taxing for her strength. This is where you belong, and don't you forget it!'

'Father is quite right!' Charlotte agreed, as Gerard went to open the shop that day. 'If anyone is going to these grand houses, it should be me! After all, I am the daughter of the house. You are only my cousin, a penniless one at that! I don't see why you should get all the attention and praise.'

Eleanor stared at her. She felt upset by Charlotte's words.

'I work hard for your father, Charlotte. You know I do, and I have tried to interest you and teach you about our trade, but you prefer to sit around pressing flowers and stitching your sampler.'

'Well, I've had enough of being in the background,' Charlotte cried peevishly. 'I'm going to ask Papa if I can become the one in charge of our shop. And I'm going to call it a salon. Shop is too middle-class. I'll be the one who says who does what. There'll be no more of you leaving all the hard work to me. I'll be the one who goes to see our customers.'

Eleanor felt dismayed. She had wanted Charlotte to take a greater share in the daily running of the business but she wasn't sure she liked the idea of Charlotte stepping so readily into her shoes.

'And you said you would teach me about shoemaking, but you are never here to do it!' she went on.

Charlotte's voice was still complaining, but Eleanor made an effort to be patient with her.

'We'll make a start today,' she offered.

It would be to their advantage if each of them was capable of the task, even if that meant Charlotte would be out with their customers whilst she was left in the shop. The thought wasn't pleasing, but Eleanor knew from experience that Charlotte would persist unceasingly with her arguments until her father agreed.

Charlotte trailed around after Eleanor throughout the morning, plucking at bootlaces, sighing loudly at every new snippet of information and finally collapsing on to one of the chairs set out for their wealthy customers.

'I do declare, Eleanor, you make heavy weather of it all. Do you imagine that our clients really wish to know all this balderdash?'

Eleanor gazed at her in exasperation.

'No, Charlotte, I don't!'

'Then why?'

'You have to know it, Charlotte! And you need to spend time in the workshop. Then you will know how each cut of the leather shapes the shoe, how it must be stitched, what are its strengths or weaknesses. You need to have an eye for colour, to know which colours or shades can be put together and which must be kept separated. You need to know . . . '

'Spare me, Eleanor! Our customers know what they want. All you need to do is agree with them. Whilst you were out the other day, I simply agreed with Mistress Garner that those tan shoes would be ideal for her and she purchased them straight away. Father was delighted. They have been on our shelf for ages.'

Eleanor pressed her lips together in exasperation.

'They are far too narrow for Mistress

Garner's foot. They will pinch her feet dreadfully.'

'Then she will return all the sooner to buy some more to replace them.'

'If she returns at all.'

'Fiddlesticks! Anyway, Mistress Dalton complimented me on my knowledge of dancing slippers. She bought four pairs yesterday. You should have seen her. She was wearing the most beautiful sapphire necklace.'

Charlotte's mouth turned down at the corners.

'I don't see why I can't wear jewellery like that! You would think Papa would wish me to be adorned in a more suitable manner, wouldn't you? It will be my birthday soon. I'm sure Papa will oblige me, if I ask it of him.'

She stood up and twirled around.

'Oh, I can just imagine it. I shall be quite beautiful wearing a sparkling necklace! A handsome prince will come into the shop and see me, and fall in love with me instantly and whisk me away from here.'

Eleanor couldn't help smiling at her. She was honest enough to admit to the same romantic notions within herself. She sighed. She often felt as though she would be dreaming her dreams for ever, and waiting for ever for that magical moment when the man of her dreams would come into her life. He didn't have a face as yet, or did he? Quite unbidden, the handsome face of Jeremy Stansfield appeared in her mind. He did have a magnetic aura about him. She remembered the intense blue of his eyes and blushed to imagine them once more looking into her own.

How foolish she was! Even if she ever met him again, he would have no memory of her. He was far above her reach, but she could have her dreams, couldn't she?

Whilst serving one or two customers with small orders, Eleanor kept a watchful eye on her cousin. She was flitting about in front of the counter making a grand show of being busy, whilst doing absolutely nothing other than arrange and rearrange their display of shoes. Gerard was pleased to see her there.

'I knew she'd come round to it, given enough time,' he whispered in Eleanor's ear. 'See what a delightful sight she is. Our customers will eat out of her hand, she's so pretty. And she is the rightful one to take her dear mamma's place,' he added, somewhat guiltily, she thought.

Eleanor pressed her lips together. Charlotte was pretty, far prettier than herself. It was a fragile beauty that seemed as though a puff of wind would dispel it. Well, it was no use comparing herself to Charlotte! Charlotte would win hands down in a contest of beauty, but what about in the realm of usefulness? Surely she had the edge there.

At the end of the week, they had made quite a good profit, and it wasn't unnoticed by Gerard.

'Well done, the pair of you!' he complimented them. 'You have both worked well. I'm particularly pleased with you, Charlotte. Growing up to be quite a young lady, you are. And I noticed that you have written up nearly as many sales as Eleanor.'

He slipped an arm around her shoulders.

'I have a good mind to give you a gift to show you how pleased I am. What would you like, eh?'

He smiled fondly down at her, enjoying the feeling of benevolence his gesture gave him. Charlotte gave pretence of careful consideration, her brow puckered in thought.

'I know! Oh, Papa! Do say I may! I would love a sapphire necklace, Papa, and it's nearly my birthday. It could do as a present for both, so it isn't too extravagant, is it?'

Gerard covered his momentary dismay at the cost of the chosen gift with a hearty laugh.

'Just like your mother! She couldn't resist her fine baubles! Yes, you may have it, daughter, for you remind me so much of her!'

Charlotte squealed with delight and jumped up to plant a kiss on her father's cheek.

'Oh, thank you, Papa! And I'll work ever so hard for you. You'll soon wonder how you managed without me.'

Eleanor wondered if her uncle would offer her a gift, too, but he made no move to do so. She wouldn't have chosen a necklace like Charlotte. She would have asked for a remnant of taffeta from the fabric shop along the street, maybe the end of a roll, where the length was too short for display. She would have chosen a dark colour, dark green or blue or deep crimson, and would have asked Sally to help her to make it up into a fine day gown.

But Gerard was already reaching for his outdoor coat for his nightly visit to the local tavern, his generosity over for the day. Eleanor couldn't help feeling disappointed. She had worked twice as hard as Charlotte.

As soon as Gerard had made his departure, Charlotte announced that she was going to her bedroom to sketch a picture of the sort of necklace she wanted. Eleanor was glad she had arranged to meet Sally at the Assembly Rooms. She needed something to cheer her spirits.

Sally was delighted to see her.

'It's my evening off,' she announced. 'Mistress Dudley has been throwing out some of her old gowns and has said I might have this one.'

She held up a dark blue taffeta gown.

'She says I've to remove all the lace and fripperies, and, of course, I'll have to cut out this tear.'

She held out the side to reveal the torn section.

'I don't know where she thinks I'll be able to wear it. Still, it's a lovely gown, isn't it?'

'You'd look pretty enough to go to the ball in that!' Eleanor exclaimed, her eyes dancing with merriment. 'Why don't you? I'm sure you'd get away with it! Didn't you say Mistress Dudley has a cupboard full of wigs? And you know how to do her make-up! Just think, a princess for a night!'

'I wouldn't dare!' Sally gasped, then she grinned mischievously. 'But you could! Go on! I dare you!'

Eleanor stared at her. She had only been joking when she made the light-hearted suggestion, never thinking for one moment that Sally would agree to it, let alone turn the tables on her. As the reality of Sally's dare sank in, she swung from incredulous hope to terrified dread. She couldn't! Could she?

She felt as though she had stopped breathing, though her heart was pounding loudly. Her lips parted. They felt dry. She moistened them with the tip of her tongue.

'Sally! Are you serious?'

Sally's face sobered.

'I wasn't,' she admitted, 'but I don't see why not! What a lark! Go on! Do it, Eleanor. Just think, you'll actually be down there amongst all that finery. Go on! I know you want to.'

Eleanor let out her breath.

'I'd love it, but dare I? What would happen if I were discovered? Would I be hauled before the magistrates?'

'Nah! You'd just be flung out on the street! No, no! I'm joking!' Sally said as Eleanor jumped to her feet in agitation. 'Sit down, Eleanor. Let's think it through! You are a similar build to me, so I'll be able to make over the gown once you've worn it, so you don't need to think you'll be taking anything of mine. We can soon take it in to make it smaller.'

'What about my hair? Has Mistress Dudley really got a cupboard full of wigs?'

'Yes. Powdered white bouffant wigs are only just going out of fashion. You can either wear one of those, or one of her dark brown ones. Even the dashing Lord Stansfield won't recognise you!'

Eleanor had told Sally about her encounter with the debonair lord. She now wished she hadn't.

'Does he come here very often?' she asked as the memory of his blue eyes made her heart race.

'Mm. He's what's known as a good catch so he is a welcome guest at any rout, and he does have an eye for a pretty face. I've heard Mistress Dudley describe him as a bit of a rake. But she always says it fondly, so I'm not so sure she means it.'

'I wouldn't count on it, the way he was dallying with Lady Lavinia that first time I was here. They wanted everyone to notice. So he is obviously quite disreputable. He cared nothing for Lady Lavinia's reputation, and the French girl I told you about has caught his eye. I would say he is a scoundrel.'

'In other words, he's every woman's dream! Let's show 'em, eh? They say you can't make a silk purse out of a sow's ear, but we can have a mighty good try at it!'

'And I'll learn the dance steps. I've already got the hang of some of them, just by watching the dancers. I dance in the shop when no-one is there. Yes, I'll do it! Oh, Sally! Just think, I'll be a countess! That's what I'll be. A countess for a night!'

The thought of Adèle's enchanting accent sprang unbidden to her mind.

'No! I know who I'll be! I'll be a French émigrée!'

Her perceived lack of understanding would cover any tricky questions she might be asked and her pretended French accent would detract from her less-than-perfect attempts to emulate the mode of speech of the English high society. Her eyes sparkled brightly.

'I shall bewitch everyone with my broken accent and all the young men shall fall hopelessly in love with me!'

It took them a few weeks to prepare everything for the grand night, as they called it. If Sally was on duty, she spent the time watching the dancers, with an ear alert for any intruders to her balcony. Other evenings, when Sally was off duty, they sewed away at the midnight-blue gown, taking in its seams, shortening its length and fitting it to Eleanor's body as closely as a well-fitting glove.

On their chosen evening, her heart hammering with excitement, Eleanor's feet tripped lightly along the streets once more to the side door of the Golders Lane Assembly Rooms. She was already wearing her borrowed gown, having decided that there was enough for Sally to do, arranging her hair and doing her make-up.

Sally was waiting.

'Quick! I haven't got long! Mistress Dudley is already downstairs greeting our guests. She will be returning for a dab of powder before long. I don't want her to miss me.'

Sally hustled Eleanor towards the stair as she spoke. Eleanor lifted the hem of her skirts and sped lightly up the flight of steps to the second floor, excitement mounting with each step.

'Did you get away all right? Nobody saw you, did they?' Sally asked.

'Yes, Charlotte did!' she replied as they were hurrying along a carpeted corridor upstairs. 'I thought I'd got away with it,' Eleanor continued. 'Uncle Gerard had gone to the tavern and Tabitha was busy in the kitchen. Charlotte was supposedly having a quiet evening drawing, but she must have guessed something was afoot. I'm afraid I told her an untruth.'

She bit her lower lip for a moment, then gurgled with laughter.

'I told her we were going to tease some of the other serving maids, to see if they could be fooled into thinking I really was a fine lady!'

'Well, it's not much different, is it? Except the ones we are teasing are the big nobs! What did she say?'

They had reached the far end of the corridor, where Sally pushed open the door, ushering Eleanor inside.

'Well, of course, she wanted to come. I didn't dare let her. She would have ruined it for us.'

'Will she betray you to her father?'

'She said not. I promised her that she could try the gown on before I give it back to you. I hope that's all right.'

She seated herself on the stool in front of the mirror, hardly able to keep still as Sally slipped a small cape around her neck to protect her gown from the make-up. Deftly, Sally applied the face powder. She lightly brushed some rouge on to her cheeks, whisking away any excess.

'Close your eyes!'

She applied powder to Eleanor's closed eyelids, skilfully adding a fine line of charcoal along the base line of her lashes.

'Look up!' she commanded. 'This will make your eyelashes look longer and darker.'

She again applied a brush with quick, expert movements.

'Now, your lips. Open your mouth slightly. There! Press your lips together. That helps the paint to set. Now a small patch on your cheekbone, just here, I think. Yes, that's perfect.'

She picked up a hand mirror.

'Right! What do you think?'

Eleanor stared into the mirror, hardly able to grasp that the face reflected there was her own. She gasped, firstly in awe, then in delight.

'Is that really me?'

She raised a hand to touch her cheek. It was her, all right! She could see her fingers lightly caressing her cheek. She didn't look real! Her fingers clutched instinctively at the golden locket. Usually, it was hidden beneath her clothes, but, tonight, it lay against her pale skin. She felt pleased about that. Somehow, the sight and feel of it gave her courage. Sally reached out and took up the wig.

'Now for this! Sit still!'

She placed the wig firmly on Eleanor's head, slipping in some small clips to anchor it securely to Eleanor's own hair.

'You'll feel a bit hot in this but it can't be helped. If it gets too hot, find a cool place, such as in one of the ante-rooms. Whatever you do, don't take it off. You'd give everyone a fright.'

Eleanor looked in the mirror again. She looked entirely different. There was no sign of her own hair. Sally was right. No-one would recognise her.

'Now, put on your dancing slippers,' Sally urged her.

Eleanor's heart began to thump erratically again. Never in her wildest dreams had she really thought that she would ever be dressed so finely, and going to a ball! All she needed now was the handsome prince!

'Oh, Sally!'

She almost lost her nerve. What if she were discovered? It would be so embarrassing. But, if she pulled out now, she would never forgive herself. To have had the chance, and not use it — unthinkable!

'You'll do fine!' Sally reassured her. 'And remember all I told you. Don't stand alone. No gentleman would dare approach you. Try to position yourself between two chaperones with a number of charges, then the young men will assume you belong to one or the other, and the chaperones will both think you are with the other! And flutter your fan, like this.'

Sally demonstrated the action, then handed it to Eleanor.

'And remember, smile brightly, but talk only a little. And don't stay too late! Your uncle will be angry if he finds out.'

That thought sent a chill running down Eleanor's back. Uncle Gerard had very strong views on morality and a woman's place in Society, but she consoled herself with the thought that he would worry more about Charlotte than herself. Lately, he had allowed her out without Tabitha on a number of occasions, but, even so, this escapade would anger him tremendously if he ever heard whisper of it. She hoped Charlotte kept her silence.

'Come on. It's time to go.'

Sally opened the door and they stepped once more into the corridor.

'I'll put your cloak in that cupboard I

showed you downstairs.'

They retraced their steps along the corridor and down one flight of stairs.

'This is as far as I dare take you. You know the way to the balcony from here. Wait until you see some others going down the wide staircase and follow them down.'

She squeezed Eleanor's hand.

'Good luck! Enjoy yourself!'

She opened the door and pushed Eleanor forward gently on to the wide balcony and closed the door behind her. Eleanor was on her own!

She tiptoed forwards to the edge of the balcony, her heart beating swiftly. The small orchestra was playing a tune that she remembered as being one of the tunes for the minuet and, yes, there they were, stepping and bowing, fingers touching, making all the movements of the dance.

Quite without thought, Eleanor began to move in time to the music, stepping her way along the carpeted balcony, conscious only of the sound of the music and the delightful swish of her skirt as it brushed against her legs. Her eyes almost closed, she held out her hand, her fingers hovering in the copied position of the ladies below.

A responsive touch on her fingers was slow to percolate into her realm of fantasy and when it did, her eyes flew open in sudden shock. The handsome face of Lord Stansfield was smiling down at her.

She felt as though her heart had stopped. All of her dreams about him faded into insignificance beside the reality of his presence. Her fingers flew to cover her mouth and she made a great effort to take control of herself.

'I'm sorry, my lord! I . . . I didn't expect . . . '

Lord Stansfield made his bow, the folds of snow-white lace falling over his wrist as he flourished his hand in front of her.

'At your service, dear lady!' he said, taking hold of her fingers and leading her in dance steps farther along the balcony as he spoke. 'But you shouldn't be dancing up here!'

Oh, dear! Was she discovered before she had even begun? But his face was smiling and she drew courage from the look of admiration that shone from his eyes. He didn't appear to recognise her from their previous encounter, which had taken place not more than a few yards away from the spot where they were now standing.

'I . . . I thought to practise,' she stammered.

She recalled how different she now looked and, at the same time, remembered her intended charade.

'Ze steps I practise a leetle before I dance down zaire, monsieur,' she lisped softly.

She dropped her eyes and glanced up at him through her thickened lashes, aware of a faint warmth on her cheeks as she did so.

'Then, you must allow me to practise with you.' He smiled. 'Though I am sure that your steps are as perfect as those of any other lady here.'

Eleanor grew more confident. He thought her a lady! She fluttered her fan as Sally had shown her.

'We 'ave not been introduced, monsieur. I should not . . . '

Lord Stansfield bowed again.

'Then, allow me to introduce myself. My name is Jeremy Stansfield, and you are?'

Eleanor dimpled, as she dropped her eyes and curtsied, beginning to enjoy herself.

'Elois Favier, monsieur.'

'You are French, mademoiselle?'

His voice held some surprise and his eyes narrowed slightly as he looked at her more directly, too directly for Eleanor's comfort! She dropped her glance and tried to appear sad and helpless, as she had seen Adèle when she spoke of her home.

'I . . . er . . . do not like to speak of it, monsieur. Eet ees too . . . '

She didn't know any French to speak

of, and was supposed not to know much English!

'Dangerous?' he said.

'Oui, monsieur.'

Phew! That was close. She hoped he didn't know much French! He would uncover her deception in no time if he chose to speak in that language. She was beginning to wonder if she had been wise to pretend to be someone so different from herself. Suddenly it wasn't as simple as she had thought. Nerves made her chatter on.

'Zat ees ze word I look for, monsieur.'

He inclined his head gravely.

'You are quite right to fear the danger, mademoiselle. These are dangerous times, for one in your position.'

Eleanor looked at him sharply. Was there a hint of laughter in his voice? But, no. His face was serious, his eyes offering concern. If only he would look at her like that yet knowing her true status. The impossibility of that shook her out of her pensive mood.

'I weel be careful, monsieur. T'ank you for your warning.'

She smiled at him again and was rewarded by an answering smile that almost melted her inside.

'Shall we proceed?' he suggested, taking hold of her hand again.

Eleanor nodded and they took several measured steps along the balcony. Her heart was pounding again. Everything was so lovely. How would she ever be content again to be merely Eleanor Faversham, shoemaker's niece?

'You make a dainty step, Mademoiselle Favier! I had better book my two dances now while your card is still free.'

Lord Stansfield's voice broke into her thoughts and she fluttered her fan as they paused. The music had stopped and the floor down below was clearing of its dancers. As the meaning of the words sunk in they brought a startled gasp to her lips.

'But, of course!'

Her hands shaking, Eleanor brought out the folded dance-card that Sally had given her. She watched eagerly as his pencil hovered.

'May I escort you into supper, Mademoiselle Favier?'

He looked enquiringly at her.

'Er . . . yes,' she stammered.

She hadn't intended staying that long, but why not? Her uncle would think her abed and she would be able to creep in quietly.

Lord Stansfield signed his name, but not his title, by two of the dances, one in about an hour's time and the one just before supper. Maybe he, too, wished to dance incognito. Eleanor felt happier about that. She could allow herself to dream further of plain Jeremy Stansfield, whereas Lord Stansfield would be out of her reach for ever.

Jeremy took hold of her hand and they moved towards the top of the grand staircase that led down to the ballroom floor. She was conscious that many eyes were upon them. So what? For all they knew, she was equal in rank to any of them. When she risked glancing up at her escort, he was giving her such looks of admiration that she felt quite heady.

'Where is your chaperone, mademoiselle?' he asked as they reached the bottom of the staircase.

Eleanor's breath caught as she cast her eyes hastily about her. She needed to be positioned near a sizeable group of people, Sally had advised her, so that she wouldn't be obviously on her own.

'Just over zaire, monsieur,' she murmured, indicating a group of young ladies by a nearby pillar.

Although she felt reluctant to be left by him, she needed time on her own to assimilate the past ten minutes or so. Her head was whirling with the sight and scents around her, and the near presence of this charismatic man. Taking a deep breath, she smiled at him over the top of her extended fan.

'T'ank you, monsieur.'

'Enchanté, mademoiselle.'

He bowed over her hand and then bowed in the direction of one of the chaperones seated nearby. Eleanor watched him depart, now apprehensive again. She felt as though everyone must know she was acting a part. It was only the memory of her unrecognisable reflection in the mirror upstairs that gave her the courage to stand her ground. She looked no different from the variety of young ladies around her, except that they seemed to know each other, whereas she knew no-one.

Who would be her next partner? Would any of these fashionable, young men desire to dance with her? What if no-one else did? But she needn't have worried! Her entrance to the ballroom on the arm of the most sought-after beau of the moment made every eligible young man determined to dance with her and her card was filled within moments of being left alone.

She was gratified to notice how captivated her partners seemed to be, and hoped she wasn't being too deceitful with her pseudo-French accent. After listening to Adèle over the previous few weeks, she found it remarkably easy to adopt the accent as long as nobody probed too deeply! She had just raised her fan to cool her cheeks, when a voice spoke in her ear.

'May I have the honour of leading you on to the floor, Mademoiselle Favier?'

Eleanor whirled around. It was Jeremy Stansfield again! He made an elaborate bow, flourishing his right hand extravagantly across his body. Her heart pounded as she fanned her cheeks to hide her sudden agitation. Had he realised her earlier deceit? Oh, what had she to lose? He wouldn't denounce her in so public a place, she was sure. A smile tugged at the corners of his mouth and tiny laughter lines crinkled at the edges of his eyes. Maybe Mistress Dudley had described him as a rake, but he was a remarkably handsome one! Suddenly confident with the headiness of her success so far, she dropped into a curtsey.

'Monsieur,' she murmured, her eye-lashes fanning across her rosy cheeks as she lowered her eyes demurely.

A gurgle of laughter seemed to spiral upward through her body. Oh, she would remember this evening until the day she died!

Eleanor knew she was playing with fire, but the challenge of his reputation and the undisputed looks of envy from nearby young ladies sent her commonsense whirling out of the windows that had been opened to let in some of the cool evening air. With a slight inclination of her beautifully-coiffured head, she accepted his offered arm, laying her fingers lightly upon it as he led her on to the floor. This was more intoxicating than their dance upstairs, or was it that the atmosphere had already unsettled her senses? Whatever, it was as though she were floating on air, her feet performing steps they hadn't even learned.

Lord Stansfield spoke little, of which she was thankful, but what little he did say was murmured quietly in her ear and, from some deep place of her own, she answered in like manner. It was as if words were not needed. Her steps were now more confident. All her previous partners faded from her memory. Every time the moves brought them face to face, Lord Stansfield's eyes were burning into her own.

It was with some degree of surprise that she eventually discovered herself being deposited again near her chosen chaperone. His eyes held hers, as she sought to quell the rapid beat of her heart. He swept his right arm in an elaborate gesture and bowed low before her. She then watched him thread his way through the crowd and although he didn't know it, he was taking her heart with him.

4

The retreating figure of Lord Stansfield gave no hint that their parting was as devastating to him as to Eleanor. She felt bewildered by the sudden overwhelming loss that his withdrawal from her side created within her.

She had never been in love. How could she have? She had never met any personable young men! And was it truly love she felt now? How could she know? All she knew was that her life would never be the same again and, although her heart was singing with the joy of her love, it was also breaking with the hopelessness of it.

The supper dance was announced and Eleanor knew that she couldn't face it. He had recognised her delight in him, she was sure. He was a man of the world, whereas she was a simple shop girl. She would be no match for his charm. She couldn't bear it.

Despising herself for her lack of courage, Eleanor fled from the ballroom. She vaguely remembered the directions Sally had given her and hurried in that direction, avoiding eye contact with anyone who impeded her escape. Her feelings of loss made her aware that she had been playing with fire. No-one else could be blamed for her aching heart, only herself. She shouldn't have agreed to attend the ball.

She would work hard, she decided. She would pour all her life and energy into building up her uncle's business and make him proud of her, and she would teach Charlotte all she knew about footwear that they could work together in harmony.

She found the cupboard containing her cloak and outdoor shoes and hurriedly put them on, then removed the wig and the numerous clips that held her own hair close to her scalp, running her fingers through the flattened curls. She felt relieved to be free of it. Apart from the taffeta gown, she was now herself, Eleanor Faversham. No more of that French émigrée nonsense! She had learned her mistake in trying to infiltrate the higher echelons of Society. She was a shop-girl, nothing more!

No-one was there to witness her flight, for which she was thankful. She thought of Jeremy Stansfield searching amongst the crush of young ladies to claim her for the supper dance and regretted any loss of pride he might be suffering. No doubt he would soon find a replacement, and would be far better off than if she had remained, deceiving him further. He would recover his pride, with plenty of eager volunteers to flatter his bruised ego.

The streets were almost deserted as Eleanor hurried along, lifting the hem of her skirt to save it from being too dirtied by the city grime and it was only as she approached the door to their living-quarters behind the shop that she began to feel any apprehension about her late return. She took the key from the pocket of her cloak and inserted it into the lock. It turned easily but when she lifted the latch the door wouldn't open. Charlotte hadn't undone the bolts! Now what was she to do?

She stepped back a pace, wondering whether or not she could throw something at Charlotte's window to alert her to her return but, as she did so, she heard the sound of the bolts being withdrawn.

'Oh, thank goodness!' she gasped as the door opened.

Her smile faded, however. It wasn't Charlotte who had opened the door for her. It was her uncle. She stared at him in dismay.

'Uncle! I wasn't . . . I didn't . . . '

'Inside, if you please, miss!'

Her uncle's face was thunderous.

'Is this how you repay me after all these years? I should have known there were traits of your mother in you, for all I hoped otherwise!'

'I'm sorry, Uncle. I didn't mean any

harm. It was a sudden whim, a dare.'

No, she couldn't blame Sally. She must take the responsibility herself.

'I wanted to taste the better things of life, just to see what it was like.'

Gerard pulled her forward, his lips curling in derision.

'You look like a painted harlot!' he shouted at her, then wrenched open her cloak, revealing the low décolletage of her gown. 'And is this how you sold yourself? You disgust me, girl! How can I have been so mistaken in you? But, no more!'

'No, Uncle Gerard! It was just a dance at the ball. I didn't do anything immoral. It was for fun!'

'Fun! My niece dressed as a trollop and you call it fun! What temptations have you beguiled Charlotte with?'

'Nothing, Uncle. Charlotte had no part in it, apart from promising to open the door for me, honestly.'

'And what was her reward to be, tell me that?'

'I said she might try on the gown,

just to see what it would be like! Nothing more!'

'You are right about that! There will be nothing more! First thing in the morning, you will leave this house!'

His shoulders sagged as he spoke the words, his face portraying sadness as well as anger. Eleanor clasped hold of his arm.

'Leave? Uncle, I have nowhere to go. You can't mean it!'

Gerard shook off her hand.

'I do mean it. I won't have Charlotte sullied by you. Wasn't it bad enough to incite her interest, without involving her in your deceit? I am only thankful that she is of such a sensitive nature that she felt compelled to confess her reluctant involvement to me.'

'But, Uncle, I've done nothing very wrong. I know I shouldn't have borrowed this gown and gone to the ball but I didn't mean any harm, truly I didn't. I won't ever do it again, I promise.'

Eleanor was desperate. He couldn't

throw her out. Where would she go? There was no-one with whom she could stay, not even temporarily. What was she to do?

Gerard shook his head, his face clearly depicting his abhorrence of the evening's events.

'Get that paint washed off you and get to bed. Be thankful I am not casting you out right this minute. Wait!' he added as she moved towards the kitchen where she knew she would find some water.

'Yes?'

Suddenly she was hopeful of a second chance, but her uncle just held out his hand.

'Give me Charlotte's necklace then I may return it to her in the morning.'

'Necklace?' Eleanor queried. 'You mean her sapphires?'

She shook her head numbly.

'I haven't got it. I haven't worn it. What do you mean?'

'Don't add theft to your behaviour, Eleanor. Charlotte said you asked for a loan of her necklace, to match the colour of your gown. She said you threatened to involve her in the deceit of all this if she refused to comply with your request.'

He passed a hand wearily across his face.

'Don't compound your sin by denying it, or have you already disposed of it? You knew what a price it could fetch. I demand it now. The necklace or the money.'

Eleanor was horrified by the accusation.

'I have neither, Uncle! Charlotte is telling lies. I haven't had her necklace. Why would I need a necklace when I have my locket? Let me call Charlotte down to explain the truth of it.'

She moved towards the staircase but Gerard pulled her back.

'You will have no more contact with my daughter, Eleanor. You are a thief, just like your mother.'

Eleanor paled at the statement.

'My mother, a thief? I don't believe it!'

'That locket and some other jewellery we sold, how else did she come by them if not by stealing? Stolen from her mistress, no doubt. That was probably why she ran away, and enslaved my brother by her witchery.'

'It was my mother's own locket. She told me so. It is all I have left of her.'

The accusation slashed a cold cut deep within her. Her mother couldn't have been a thief. Her papa would never have loved a thief. She felt her knowledge of her own innocence strengthen her conviction of her mother's innocence. She raised her head and glared unflinchingly at her uncle.

'If you believe me to be a thief, then there is no more to be said. You may be assured that I will leave first thing in the morning! Good-night!'

Her back ramrod straight, she made her way upstairs, all thought of washing her face forgotten. She didn't know where she was to go, or how she might support herself, but she couldn't stay here, not where her cousin had maligned her name and where her uncle believed the lie.

But, where was she to go?

Eleanor slept fitfully, her mind running over the events of the latter part of the evening, and over Charlotte's unfounded accusation. How could her cousin have lied so, and why? They had had their differences but nothing to warrant this.

As soon as the first streaks of dawn lit the sky, Eleanor rose from her bed and parcelled her few belongings. There wasn't much — a couple of dresses and some undergarments. She was careful to take nothing that her uncle might lay claim to, adding to his charge of theft. She felt very bitter towards her cousin, unable to rationalise her accusation. She hadn't realised that Charlotte hated her so deeply.

The blue taffeta gown she wrapped separately. She would leave it with Tabitha to return it to Sally at some opportune time. The thought of a possible position there crossed her mind, but was dismissed instantly. She couldn't bear to think of people who knew her thinking she was a thief, and she was sure the accusation would somehow reach there if she moved so near to home. She gulped. In five more minutes, she wouldn't have a home!

She paused outside the door of Charlotte's room. She even raised her hand to knock, but let it fall again. What was the point? The damage was done. What could she hope to achieve?

Tabitha was in the kitchen, tearfully wrapping some bread, cheese and apples into a cloth.

'Oh, Miss Eleanor, I don't know what's happening, but I heard all the shouting. I couldn't let you go without seeing you and giving you something to take with you. What a to-do there was, even before you came home. What have you been getting up to? Such words I heard, as I never thought to hear about you, and your mamma, God rest her soul.'

Eleanor hugged her, her tears spilling

down her cheeks.

'I've done nothing very bad, Tabitha, a little foolish, perhaps. But I didn't steal Charlotte's necklace. She has made that up for some reason. Uncle Gerard says my mother was a thief, but I'm sure she wasn't.'

Tabitha wiped her eyes on the edge of her apron, sniffing indelicately.

'Where will you go, Miss Eleanor? What will you do?'

'I don't know, Tabitha. If all else fails, I will have to find a workhouse, but I will try to get some work before I try that. Maybe another shopkeeper will take me on, or I could try to become some sort of maid. I'm not afraid of hard work.'

'Take care, Miss Eleanor. It can be a cruel world out there. Don't trust no-one until you know differently. And, Miss Eleanor, try to get word to me that you're all right. I'll miss you, I will. And so will Miss Charlotte when she finds out that she's to do all your work as well as her own.'

Eleanor sniffed back her tears and forced out a tremulous smile.

'I'll try, Tabitha.'

Creaking floorboards above their heads drew their eyes upwards. Eleanor held out the package containing Sally's gown and hastily explained to Tabitha what she hoped she would do for her. Tabitha took it out of her hands, agreeing to her request.

'I'd best be off, Tabitha. I've no wish to see my uncle again.'

Eleanor leaned forward and dropped a kiss on Tabitha's cheek.

'Remember me in your prayers and take care of yourself. Don't let Charlotte work you too hard, for I'm sure she'll try.'

She took the parcel of food out of Tabitha's hands and left swiftly. She wanted to put as much distance as she could between her and her now estranged family. Outside, the streets were beginning to fill. The city never really slept, she supposed. Early-morning traders were transporting their goods and street cleaners were at work. Eleanor hurried past them all. She had no plan formed in her mind.

By the end of the afternoon, her optimism was fading fast. No-one, it seemed, needed a helping hand with their business, or, if they did, none was willing to take on a tired-looking girl with no references.

She eventually found herself in the market place, where stallholders shouted their wares and grubby urchins ran about, trying to entice a farthing or two from anyone who looked likely to have money to spare. She had eaten her bread and cheese earlier and now had only an apple left. She was reluctant to eat it too soon, for then she would have nothing.

Weary in mind and body, she seated herself on the uneven steps of the stone cross in the middle of the market, near to despair. After a moment or two, she felt able to raise her head and look around. The crowds had thinned now, leaving the stragglers who hoped for a bargain or two and the stallholders beginning to pack their surplus stock into wicker baskets.

A sudden shout of, 'Stop thief!' drew her attention. An irate stallholder was shaking his fist, trying to get past his upturned basket of oranges, trying in vain to stop a young boy who was running away with an orange clutched in each hand. More oranges were spilling on to the cobbled ground and rolling in all directions. As the boy drew level with Eleanor, he turned and made a rude gesture to the stallholder, chortling with glee at the mayhem he had caused. He appeared to be more hungry than wicked, Eleanor thought, conscious of her own unpremeditated plight.

She could see a large man approaching the boy with his hand outstretched to capture him.

'Run, boy!' she shouted, before she had time to think.

The boy turned towards her, sidestepping the man's hand.

'Here, catch!' he called, tossing an orange to her.

Eleanor gasped, her hands automatically rising to catch hold of the orange. The boy sped on his way, grinning delightedly and still calling rude comments over his shoulder. The dispersing crowd soon swallowed him up and the large man gave up the chase. Eleanor stood, intending to return the orange to its erstwhile owner but halted as she took in his furious expression, directed at her!

'Hey, you!'

The man was gesticulating in her direction. Eleanor looked around. All the faces seemed hostile to her, but none seemed sure what the commotion was about. Eleanor swiftly weighed her options. One was to stay and try to explain her non-involvement, the other was to cut and run!

'You, girl!'

The second shout made up her mind for her. She whirled away and ran, not as swiftly as the boy but faster than any of her pursuers.

'Stop that girl!'

The shouts behind her spurred her feet onwards. Now, she really was a thief, she couldn't help thinking! And no-one would believe otherwise. She darted round a corner and then another, putting more distance between her and those public-spirited persons who had given chase. She found herself to be in a narrow entry, with smaller entries going off at regular intervals. As she hesitated and looked over her shoulder, she glimpsed a slight flash of orange. In the small gap to her right sat the young urchin, squatting on his haunches as cool as ice, peeling his orange. He grinned up at her.

'Either come in, miss, or run on!' he invited. 'But don't just stand there. You'll get nabbed.'

The sound of running feet sent her scurrying in beside the boy, who calmly swung the rickety gate across the opening then sat with his back against it, still eating the orange.

'You'd best eat it quick, just in case!' he advised. 'They can't do nowt without the evidence! Give it 'ere. I'll start it off for you.'

He took the orange out of her hand and sank his teeth into the peel, tearing off a chunk.

'There y'are,' he grinned, handing it back. 'Get it down yer quick!'

He wiped the back of his hand across his mouth with an appreciative sucking sound.

'That were good!'

Eleanor laughed for the first time that day.

'You'll get me into bad ways!' she joked, ripping off some more peel, until she had enough of the orange exposed to take a bite.

The refreshing taste of the juice running down her throat made her realise how thirsty she had been and she gratefully took another bite.

'Do you often do this?' she asked.

'What, pinch oranges? Yeah! Whenever I wants one. There ain't no other way, is there?'

The boy spoke in a matter-of-fact way, shrugging his shoulders.

'How do you get yer grub then?'

Eleanor's face lost its smile.

'I used to work for it,' she said grimly, 'but I was accused of stealing and got thrown out.'

'What did yer pinch?'

'Nothing, but it made no difference.'

'Where d'you live?'

'Nowhere!'

'There's a gang of us sleeps in the crypt of a church. You can join us, if yer likes. Me name's Bertie, by the way. What's yours?'

'Eleanor,' she replied hesitantly.

She didn't want to be ungrateful, but she couldn't see herself sleeping in a church with a gang of street boys. If she didn't get herself sorted with some kind of a job while she was still relatively clean, she would never get one. She stood up, automatically running her hands down her skirt to smooth out the creases. At that moment, she realised that both her hands were empty. She had left her small parcel of clothes at the stone cross when she ran away! Now, she truly had nothing!

'It might still be there,' the boy said hopefully. 'Come on. If we work our way around and come from a different direction, nob'dy will know it was us.'

Eleanor followed Bertie but their hopes of finding her parcel of clothes were disappointed. The steps of the stone cross were bare.

'Hey! You two!'

The sudden shout from across the almost deserted square made them both turn round. It was the fruit stallholder, his face still showing his anger.

'Scarper!' Bertie yelled, running swiftly across the cobbles.

Eleanor was slower to react. She heard the sound of hoof beats and the rumble of wheels on the cobblestones but her mind was distracted by the approaching figure of the stallholder. She turned to run, straight into the path of the horse and carriage. She pulled back but couldn't stop completely.

The nearness of the carriage unbalanced her and with a cry of alarm, she fell to the ground, striking her head as she landed. She felt a sharp pain dart through it, then, mercifully, all went dizzy and black.

5

Eleanor groaned and tried to sit up but felt a restraining hand against her shoulder and another under her head as she was lowered back to her lying position.

'Oh, my head,' she moaned.

'Lie still!' she heard a man's voice say. 'We need to make sure that you are unharmed, apart from your head, that is, but there is no bleeding there, so it was probably just a hard bang.'

The voice was somehow familiar but she couldn't place it. She tried to open her eyes but saw a flash of stars through her head. She tried to move.

'Lie still! I need to ascertain that you have no bones broken.'

Hands, the man's hands, she presumed, felt along Eleanor's legs carefully, then her arms and spine, causing only mild discomfort as Eleanor felt her body being turned this way and that gently.

'That appears to be satisfactory. We will lift her into my carriage and take her to her home. Here, Robson!'

Eleanor forced open her eyes and saw that the man had called to his groom, who was now holding the heads of the two magnificent greys that were pawing at the cobbles, eager to be off again.

'Yer can't do that, mister!' a boy's voice cut in.

'And who might you be, boy?'

'Bertie, mister. We're mates, me and 'er!'

'And what about my oranges?' a belligerent voice demanded.

'What about your oranges?' the man's voice drawled impatiently.

' 'Er folks have slung 'er out!'

'Her and that lad stole my oranges. I want recompense!'

The two voices had spoken simultaneously.

'What do you mean, boy?' the stranger demanded.

'She told me! Her uncle's thrown her

out. She's no job, nowhere to go. She's a lady, mister. She won't know how to live on t'streets.'

Eleanor groaned. They were talking about her! And it was all true. She couldn't go home. Her uncle, as well as this stallholder, had named her a thief, and how would she survive? The question of the owner of the voice slipped away. She tried to sit up again. She needed to get away . . . far away from anyone who knew her. And far away from this man who was towering over her! It felt like a nightmare.

'Right, boy, open the carriage door for me.'

Two strong arms swung Eleanor off the ground. She tried to protest but the movement made her head spin.

'And me, mister! We're sticking together, me and 'er. Like I said, we're mates!' Bertie's voice rang out.

'And what about my oranges?' the belligerent voice came again. 'I demand satisfaction or I'll get the law.'

Eleanor was faintly aware of the

man's voice saying, 'Take this half-sovereign and be off with you, man! Consider the matter settled or I will be the one calling the law.'

She felt herself being laid down on the upholstered carriage seat and she opened her eyes. The world had stopped spinning round and the man's face came into focus. It was Jeremy Stansfield!

'Oh, no!' Eleanor groaned, closing her eyes again.

Of all the men in London, why him? Please, God, don't let him recognise me. She couldn't bear the questions, the humiliation, the rejection, all in front of the crowd that had gathered. She struggled to sit up.

'Please, let me go! I feel so ashamed. I can't impose myself upon you.'

Bertie leaped into the carriage, pushing her back against the cushions.

'Let's be away, mister! She looks as though she's going to croak it.'

'No, I don't.'

It was a feeble protest, however. The

world was spinning round again when she tried to raise her head.

'Sit on the floor, boy! I'll sit by the young lady.'

Bertie bounced off the seat, straight up on to the opposite one.

'Cor, mister! Can I sit up there with 'im?' he asked, pointing to the driver, who had climbed into the driving seat.

'Anywhere, boy! And don't fall. I don't want another accident on my hands. Robson, watch that boy. No, young lady, don't try to speak!'

Eleanor had tried once to sit up and assure Lord Stansfield that she was all right and that he must let her depart immediately. The earnest anxiety in her eyes held his gaze. Lord Stansfield's eyes narrowed as he looked at her. Where had he seen those lovely eyes before? For a wonderful, insane moment a fleeting spark of knowledge shot through him, accompanied by a shaft of desire. He had found her!

But his joy fled instantly as his mind dismissed it as ludicrous. Was he going to see his delightful partner of the previous evening in every female who crossed his path possessing eyelashes flecked with gold?

Eleanor was aware of the intensity of Lord Stansfield's gaze as he studied her features. She allowed her eyes to slide away from Lord Stansfield's and became aware of the babble of voices around the carriage. Quite a crowd had assembled, making the most of the unusual spectacle of a man of quality having taken a young lady of uncertain means into his carriage and engaging her in what seemed to be some intensive quizzing.

Following her gaze, Lord Stansfield snapped, 'Drive on, Robson!'

'Where to, mi'lord?'

'Anywhere! One of the parks, St James, anywhere!'

Eleanor couldn't help smiling slightly as she realised that the normally suave man was ever so slightly rattled. He took his seat opposite her and she closed her eyes as the carriage jerked into motion. She needed time to think. He didn't seem to have recognised her so far. When they reached the park, she would thank him kindly for his assistance and she would go.

Her mental plans drew to an abrupt standstill. What would she do? She had nowhere to go. What would become of her? In a flash of unaccustomed despair, Eleanor sank back against the cushions.

Lord Stansfield resumed his conversation.

'There is no way I can abandon you. It was my carriage that knocked you down, though I must say, you appeared from nowhere.'

'I'm sorry to be such an inconvenience!' she snapped, suddenly refusing to be held responsible for his reckless driving. 'Maybe if you had better control of your horses the accident would never have happened.'

Lord Stansfield's eyebrows nearly disappeared under the shock of dark hair that fell disarmingly over his forehead. Eleanor swallowed hard, feeling an almost compulsive desire to reach out and smooth the unruly lock into place. She resisted the impulse. Instead, she had the grace to blush.

'I suppose I did move rather suddenly,' she confessed. 'I suddenly realised that the stallholder was about to grab hold of me and heaven knows what would have happened then. He looked very fierce.'

'So, you took the easier option of flinging yourself under my carriage?'

'I didn't have time to think. I just wanted to get away.'

'With your purloined oranges, of course!' Lord Stansfield said lightly, leaning back against his seat.

Eleanor blushed at the mildly-spoken accusation. It mattered to her that he didn't think badly of her.

'I didn't steal them. I merely tried to help Bertie make his getaway. It seemed an unequal chase, and I chose, however unwisely, to intervene.'

'And without success,' Lord Stansfield added.

'Oh, no, not at first. We made our getaway, only I dropped my parcel of clothing and I . . . we . . . decided to go back to see if it was still there.'

'Not a wise thing to do, to return to the scene of the crime,' Lord Stansfield said. 'At least, not so soon. I take it your clothes were gone?'

'Yes. Then the stallholder saw us. The rest you know.'

She spread her hands helplessly, her mind filled with the bleakness of her situation. She closed her eyes again and tried to assemble her jumbled thoughts. It was difficult to do so in such close proximity to the man opposite. With startling clarity, she could still feel the touch of his hand on hers as they danced, the fleeting warmth of his breath on her cheeks and the light of admiration in his eyes.

He had admired her, she knew, but, then, he had thought her a person of quality, a member of the disgraced

French aristocracy, perhaps, though she hadn't actually said so to him. But now, she was nothing but an unwanted inconvenience, so she might as well accept that her dream was over and she would soon be forced into the reality of her desperate state.

'What's your name?' Lord Stansfield asked suddenly.

Eleanor's eyes flew open in apprehension. She felt as though her guilt was painted on her face. Which name should she give him? Ella? Eloise? She decided to give her real name.

'Eleanor Faversham,' she said finally.

'Well, Miss Faversham, you have put me in quite a quandary. Since it was my carriage, however inadvertently, that knocked you over, I do feel some responsibility towards you. The young lad up front tells me that your uncle has cast you out of his home. Is that true?'

'Yes,' she whispered, the shame of it washing over her.

'May I ask why?'

'He, too, accused me of stealing, but

I hadn't! You must believe me!'

Suddenly, it felt imperative that he believe her.

'You seem to make a habit of being accused thus.'

His light tone belied the starkness of his words.

'What are you supposed to have stolen this time? Something of value?'

'Yes,' she replied and again, her voice was no more than a whisper. It was obvious to her that he doubted the truth of her words.

'My cousin's sapphire necklace,' she went on. 'I had admired it, but I didn't steal it. I wear my own locket. What need did I have of a necklace?'

Her hand rose to her throat, where she could feel the hardness of her locket under the high neckline of her dress. It was her one possession. Maybe she could sell it. The thought was coldly abhorrent to her. It was the one thing she had to remind her of her mother and the dreams of her origins.

The simplicity of her response made

him smile and his words seemed to be an echo of her thoughts.

'It could be sold. Was it a genuine necklace, or were the stones false?'

'Genuine,' she admitted. 'It is a lovely necklace but I didn't steal it,' she repeated. 'Truly, I didn't!'

'Could someone else have taken it? Where did your cousin keep it?'

'In her room. I think she has hidden it to get me into trouble. She is jealous of . . . of . . .'

What could she say?

'Yes?' he prompted.

'My uncle owns a shop,' Eleanor explained. 'Charlotte has never shown much interest until recently, when I began to visit some of our clients in their homes. She feels it is her right to be the prominent one, but the clients ask for me because I know how to advise them.'

'Ah!'

The brevity of his response drew her gaze to his face once more. Didn't he believe her? From the blandness of his expression she couldn't determine. His eyebrows puckered and his eyes narrowed slightly.

'Do I know you from somewhere?' he asked suddenly.

Of which encounter was he thinking? On the balcony, or holding her during the dances? Those precious, sweet moments still brought a flutter to her heart, but she couldn't for shame admit to that.

'I have visited Mistress Dudley at the Assembly Rooms, my lord,' she said quietly.

'In what circumstances?'

'My uncle owns a shoe shop. Mistress Dudley is one of our clients, and Lady Harrington. I have taken shoes and other items to them both, and other ladies of quality.'

His eyebrows puckered.

'I don't remember seeing you.'

'I have found that people of quality do not take note of those of lower classes, especially in someone else's home.'

Lord Stansfield considered the accusation so gently given. Could he in all honesty deny it? He tried to imagine the faces of some of his own parlour maids, and failed. He made a nod of agreement.

'So, you know who I am?' he asked her directly.

She nodded, her cheeks still burning. 'You are Lord Stansfield.'

'And Lady Harrington and Mistress Dudley would vouch for you?'

'Yes, I expect so, that is, unless they believe the accusation against me!'

Lord Stansfield acknowledged her amendment with a slight inclination of his head.

'So, back to my quandary. I can either take you home. No, no, let me finish,' he insisted as she began to protest. 'Or, I can take you to either of the two ladies mentioned to see if there is anything they can do for you.'

He paused, watching her reaction. Eleanor wasn't sure what her reception would be at either Harrington House or the Assembly Rooms. What would they think about the accusation of theft? Would they believe Charlotte's story or her own? Who would want to employ an accused thief? And her uncle would undoubtedly be told of her whereabouts. However badly he had treated her at present, he was the only family she had and he had given her a home for all her past years. Could she face bringing dishonour to his name?

'Or,' Lord Stansfield continued thoughtfully, 'I can take you with me to the coast.'

Eleanor's eyes opened wide. The coast? Was he about to make one of his smuggling trips? Why would he want her to go with him?

'Take me with you? But, I don't understand. Why take me with you? For what reason?'

'I can't tell you that, not yet. Tell me, have you any knowledge of being a lady's maid? You speak rather well. You have had some education?'

'A little. My mamma was . . . '

She was about to say, a lady, but her uncle's dismissal of that was still fresh in her mind.

'Mamma was a lady's maid, sir. She taught me to speak correctly and to read, write and cipher. She showed me how to set a table correctly, how to eat correctly and correct deportment.'

Lord Stansfield smiled.

'Then you are perfectly qualified for what I have in mind. Do you have any understanding of anything French?'

'French?'

She couldn't prevent the echo. Was he trying to trick her? Did he recognise her from last evening after all? She gazed at him in dismay.

'The French language,' he stated patiently.

He made a quick gesture with his hand, as if persuading himself that he had better divulge more of his plan.

'The rôle I have in mind for you is to be a temporary maid to a young French lady whom I am about to take under my wing, shall we say.'

Eleanor thought of Adèle immediately. Hadn't Lady Harrington said that Lord Stansfield was to visit her, that he had an interest in her? But, surely, she had a maid already at Lady Harrington's residence. How many young French ladies did he know?

Lord Stansfield was still awaiting her response.

'So, tell me, Miss Faversham, which is it to be?'

6

Eleanor's heart felt as though it had stopped beating. What a choice! But, did she really have a choice? It would be so humiliating to have to make all the explanations to either Lady Harrington or Mistress Dudley, and to their staff. And what if Charlotte took over her rôle in Uncle Gerard's shop and she were to make visits to their establishments and see her there in the rôle of servant? She couldn't bear it!

'I have no true knowledge of the French language,' Eleanor admitted truthfully, 'but I am sure I could be of assistance to a young French lady. I am willing to give it a try.'

'Good.'

He rose from his seat and spoke to the coachman.

'Robson, make straight for the coast.

We should be just in time for the evening tide.'

'Right y'are, m'lord! We're on our way!'

Robson sounded cheered by the return to the original plan and Bertie turned round to make a thumbs-up sign to Eleanor, his face alight with excitement. Eleanor smiled weakly. There were many questions buzzing around in her mind but she felt unable to voice them in the uncertainty of her position. If she probed too deeply, Lord Stansfield might regard her as a liability and, however illegal his activities as a smuggler might be, she had to admit to a growing anticipation of excitement herself.

Eleanor was unaware of the stirrings of interest about her within Lord Stansfield's sceptical heart. He had spent his youth and adult years as the aim of too many hopeful young ladies to succumb to a lady's fluttering eyes or beguiling manoeuvres of their fans. But Miss Faversham was making no such overtones. Could it be that her heart was engaged elsewhere?

He found it to be a refreshing change to contend with her lack of passion for him. He smiled faintly. Maybe he was losing his touch! And still, that niggling query gnawed away in the back of his mind that he had met her in some other circumstance, but when could it have been?

It was a few hours later, when they drew into the courtyard of an inn. Robson had already leaped to the ground and Bertie had followed suit.

'We're at Dover, Miss Ella,' Bertie announced excitedly. 'Cor! It even smells different, don't it? I ain't never been to the seaside before.'

Lord Stansfield was ready to hand her down from the carriage and she put her hand into his, experiencing a tremor of delight as she did so.

'Thank you,' she said crisply. 'Are we to spend the night here?'

'You are, and the lad,' Lord Stansfield informed her, equally crisply. 'I will make suitable arrangements for you, have no fear.'

He led her past the open door of the taproom into a pleasant room, where a fire blazed in the hearth and high-backed chairs flanked its sides. The windows were shuttered against the night air and the warmth from the fire filled the room. A long table ran down its centre and a number of chairs were tucked tidily around it. A bowl of fruit sat in the middle and, already, a serving girl was carrying in a platter of bread, butter and cheeses.

'You will eat a hot meal?' the landlord enquired.

His smiling face beamed upon them and Eleanor found herself smiling in return. She was feeling a little out of her depth, never having been inside any sort of hostelry before. The landlord's cheery nature put her at her ease.

'I can offer you hot, vegetable soup and fresh bread and a dish of mutton, broccoli and boiled potatoes.'

'That sounds delightful,' Eleanor told him.

She was suddenly aware of how hungry she was having eaten very little that day. It was only when she then heard Lord Stansfield ordering a room for her that she realised she had nothing to change into for her night's sleep. Lord Stansfield took the hastily whispered information in his stride.

'That will be taken care of,' he assured her. 'I have an arrangement here and Mistress Varney will help you to select garments. I have already told her what you will need. Select anything that takes your pleasure.'

Eleanor bit back her puzzled enquiry as to what he meant by an arrangement. Did Lord Stansfield often stop here with ladies who travelled without their own clothes, and in what circumstances? She glanced around, looking for a reaction from either the landlord or his wife, but saw no-one.

The maid returned with a tray of bowls of hot soup and Eleanor was pleased to be invited to be seated at the table immediately. Bertie was already tucking into a chunk of bread and Eleanor quickly joined him. She felt she feasted well, even before the hot slices of mutton, the creamy white potatoes and the bright green broccoli had been placed before them.

Bertie drank a glass of porter with relish.

'That were right good, missus,' he complimented.

Eleanor added her thanks, pleased that Bertie had been appreciative without any prompting. Lord Stansfield, along with Robson and Tom Varney, the landlord, was sitting a little apart from her and Bertie. The three men had their heads together, in earnest conversation and, when it became obvious that they were about to rise and depart, Eleanor rose also.

'No, not you and the lad,' Lord Stansfield forbade. 'Mistress Varney will attend to you. The lad will sleep down here. Don't worry. I am not abandoning you far from home. Have a good night's sleep and be ready for our departure back to London on the morrow.'

His voice was gentle and Eleanor felt a lump in her throat. Until he had said not to worry, she hadn't. Now, she wondered what there was to worry about. Was it to do with his smuggling activities? Tom Varney and Robson must be fellow-conspirators! Were they about to set off into danger? What if there was trouble and they didn't come back?

She caught Bertie's eye and mouthed the words, 'Follow them!'

Bertie nodded, his bright eyes gleaming. He slid silently out of the room in trail of the men and it was with some reluctance that Eleanor followed Mistress Varney up the stairs to the room allocated to her. It was sparsely furnished but everything looked clean and warm.

'Come with me,' Mistress Varney bade her, after drawing back the corner of the bedcovers.

Eleanor followed her into another room where there was a number of large chests and two wardrobes. Mistress Varney threw back the lid of one of the chests and began to search carefully through the contents. Eleanor could see that they were items of clothing and she was amazed when Mistress Varney lifted out some lovely dresses and undergarments.

'They are too fine for me,' she objected. 'I'm sure Lord Stansfield doesn't expect you to give me such good clothes.'

'This will suit you fine, dear,' Mistress Varney assured her.

It was a day-gown of dark red brocade, with a shawl collar. Eleanor could see at a glance that it would suit her wonderfully and the wide-brimmed hat with a shallow crown would sit delightfully on her golden hair.

'It's lovely! Can it really be mine?'

'Aye, and a few more besides. Lord Stansfield is very generous towards those he brings here, God bless him.'

Eleanor felt a stab of disappointment. All she knew was that her pleasure at receiving the garments evaporated in an instant. When Eleanor returned to her room, she had three complete outfits folded over her arm. She dispiritedly flung them on to the bed and crossed over to the small window.

It was now quite dark and the moon was shining brightly, not a favourable night for smuggling, she thought bitterly. She could hear the waves pounding against the cliffs to her right and wondered if the evening tide had brought in the contraband that Lord Stansfield hoped for. Why did he do it? Surely he had money enough without risking his life like this. Was it simply for the excitement? And why the innkeeper? Did Lord Stansfield stock his cellar with some of the spoils, thus ensuring his compliance, and his silence? Had the man no scruples?

Sounds of commotion attracted her attention, the ring of hooves on the cobbled yard, male voices shouting.

Eleanor was alarmed instantly. Were the coastguards and the excisemen here? Had they knowledge of the night's activities? Without stopping to consider her own safety, she snatched up her cloak and made her way downstairs. As she approached the taproom, she could hear Mistress Varney talking to the men, assuring them that her husband was away on business and that the inn was closed to visitors. Eleanor drew back into the shadows.

A man's voice spoke sharply.

'Spread out, men! We'll search the place!'

Eleanor gasped. She had to move swiftly. She turned and ran lightly along the dark corridor hoping it led to the outside. She felt for the latch and lifted it silently, relieved to find that the door wasn't bolted. It had probably been left as such for the men's return. Thankful that her clothes were dark, she pressed against the outer wall of the inn, recognising her surroundings as being under her window. So, the sea was slightly to the right. With a hasty glance around, she ran in that direction, hoping she would be able to find a path down to the shore.

In the moonlight she could see over the cliffs. There would be no cover once she was down there. She caught her breath. She had seen movement at the edge of the sea. There was a small boat, and three dark figures were wading out to it, unaware of their danger! She paused and looked uncertainly to the left and to the right. Which way should she go?

A sudden movement to her right made her freeze. A human shape was rising to its feet. With a gasp of relief, she realised that it must be Bertie.

'Psst! Miss Ella! Over here!' he hissed from the top of a winding cliff path. 'The boat's only just got here, miss. Shall we go and help them?'

'We're not here to help!' Eleanor said sharply. 'They're in danger! The excisemen are here! We must warn them! Come on, but be careful.'

Bertie went first. His nimble legs moved swiftly, barely pausing when rocks slid away under his feet. Eleanor followed more slowly, hampered by her skirt and unsuitable footwear. When he reached the silvery sand, Bertie was already nearing the water's edge. She heard his voice call out a warning and saw the men's bodies stiffen in response. One man broke away from the others and strode towards her. It was Lord Stansfield.

'What are you doing here? Don't you realise you are in danger?'

His voice was low but his annoyance was evident.

'I had to come! The excisemen are at the inn. They are searching the place. It won't take them long to realise that this is where the action will be.'

As if to prove her words, a shout from the cliff top rang out clearly.

'Stay where you are. We have you covered.'

Lord Stansfield uttered an oath and then grasped Eleanor's hand.

'You'll have to come with us! Quick!'

He turned back towards the sea and dragged Eleanor along with him. Bertie ran ahead and was already splashing through the shallow water. Eleanor wasn't given a chance to hesitate. The water was cold and her skirts were soon dragging heavily about her. She held them up as best she could with her free hand. A shout behind her made her look over her shoulder. A number of men were running over the sand towards them.

At that moment, they were by the boat. Lord Stansfield swept her into his arms and dumped her in the depths of the small craft. He leaped in after her and immediately the men at the oars began to pull away from the shore.

Eleanor pulled herself upright. The excisemen, or whoever they were, were wading into the sea after them. They seemed too close for comfort but the boat was making good headway. Two large men were at the oars. Lord Stansfield and Master Varney were crouching down, in the midst of a cluster of other people, one of whom was Bertie.

'Get your head down!' Lord Stansfield ordered sharply.

After a startled look at him, Eleanor did as she was told, just in time, it seemed! She heard the crack of a pistol and couldn't help a short scream. Another crack of a pistol sounded and one of the oarsmen gave a grunt of pain. Immediately, Lord Stansfield pushed him forward and took his place at the oars. The wounded man crumpled at Eleanor's side, clutching his upper arm, his face grimacing with pain.

'Lean against me,' Eleanor suggested. 'That will be more comfortable for you. Can I help you at all?'

'Nay, lass. I can manage until we're aboard the Mary Jane.'

The Mary Jane? Eleanor risked a peep over the side of the boat. Riding at anchor, not more than a hundred yards away, lay a two-masted schooner. A glance back at the shore showed the excisemen waist-high in the water, shaking their fists in fury at the timely escape.

The next moment, they were bumping alongside the schooner. Master Varney stood in the prow and threw a line which ready hands grasped hold of, drawing the rowing boat against the side of the vessel and holding it fast whilst its occupants scrambled aboard. The injured man was helped up first, then one of the people who had been huddled down in the boat near Eleanor. He spoke strange words, his accent sounding very like Adèle's.

Then Eleanor herself was assisted aboard the larger vessel. It was an undignified push-pull-and-scramble, her long skirt being a decided disadvantage. Bertie joined her next, then another foreign man, Master Varney, Lord Stansfield and, eventually, the other oarsman. Eleanor felt the schooner lean forward as the captain gave his order.

'Weigh anchor!'

In spite of the tense excitement, her heart leaped with the thrill of it. The vessel seemed to take on a life of its own, surging forward.

For a moment, she forgot why they were there and simply enjoyed the experience. A glance shoreward showed that the white cliffs of Dover were almost out of sight. The breeze blew her hair back off her face and Eleanor took a deep breath. This was wonderful!

'Are you all right?'

The voice broke into her reverie. It was Lord Stansfield. He was standing close behind her and he laid a restraining hand on her shoulder. It felt intoxicating and she couldn't help a quiver of exhilaration zip through her. Lord Stansfield's face was close to her own.

'Yes, thank you,' she breathed in reply.

For a moment her body sent her the wrong signal then she remembered! Her eyes blazed with anger as she turned towards him.

'I can't believe it! What kind of man are you that you will risk people's lives merely to experience some excitement? Haven't you enough riches, without smuggling? You are endangering not only your own life, but also the lives of your friends, if, indeed, that is what you call them.'

His right eyebrow rose quizzically, then he smiled.

'Amazing!'

'Pardon?'

'I said it's amazing!'

'What is?'

'Your eyes. In daylight they are blue. Now, in this moonlight, they look green. Or is it because you are angry, I wonder.'

'You can't possibly see the colour of my eyes in this light!' she snapped. 'Don't you dare try to trivialise my words! You have acted in a most irresponsible way and I am shocked.'

Lord Stansfield considered her words. Eleanor quailed under his scrutiny, beginning to feel that she had been far too outspoken. She forced herself to meet his gaze unflinchingly and felt a flash of success when Lord Stansfield was the one to look away first. He made pretence of flicking away some imaginary speck off his sleeve. Eleanor's lips began to curl in scorn and she was taken aback when he met her gaze again.

'What were you doing there on the beach?' he asked her sharply, ignoring her questions. 'How did the excisemen find us?'

Eleanor's breath caught in her throat.

'Are you implying that I led them to you? How dare you!'

Swallowing hard, she drew herself as tall as she could.

'I came to warn you of their presence,' she said coldly. 'The men arrived at the inn and were questioning Mistress Varney. It seemed to be the best course of action at the time. Maybe I shouldn't have bothered! You could, no doubt, have managed on your own!'

'No doubt!' Lord Stansfield echoed

dryly, inclining his head to acknowledge that he accepted her reply. 'However, your presence here presents us with a slight problem.'

'I think I can promise not to get in your way,' she said stiffly.

'It isn't that simple.'

'Why not? You mean I'm a witness to your activities? I won't tell anyone,' she faltered, suddenly afraid.

Lord Stansfield shook his head.

'That is not the problem.'

He smiled. It made him seem younger, and less hostile. Eleanor's heart flipped. This man's magnetism set her pulse racing far too easily.

'Then, what is? I'm quite happy here. I'm enjoying it, really. I won't have a fit of the vapours, or anything like that.'

Lord Stansfield laughed.

'I'm sure you won't!' he agreed. 'No, the fact is, only part of our, shall we say, cargo arrived.'

Eleanor remembered the conversation she had overheard on the balcony of the Assembly Rooms. She felt appalled that he wasn't satisfied with the danger encountered so far!

'Huh! All of this is your precious cargo! Are you willing to risk men's lives again for a few more barrels?'

Too late, she saw Lord Stansfield's eyes narrow slightly.

'I think, madam, you know more than you have admitted to!'

He gripped her chin in his hand and held her firmly, his eyes hard and challenging. Eleanor trembled again, aware that her guilty thoughts would be mirrored on her face, but she couldn't admit to having overheard him. She hadn't meant to, and hadn't passed on the information.

'I just used the phrase you yourself have spoken.'

His glare of steel was replaced by one of puzzlement.

'Who precisely are you, Miss Faversham? I feel I know you, yet I don't!'

His face was very close now. Eleanor could feel his breath fanning her cheeks. Now that he was no longer stern-faced, she wasn't afraid. He couldn't identify her. Only her eyes had remained uncovered or unchanged. Feeling emboldened by her anonymity, she smiled teasingly.

'Every woman has some mystery about her, my lord. I may not be as grand as the ladies you meet socially but, underneath, I am as feminine as they are.'

She tried to glance down coyly, but his hand prevented her and she was forced to raise her eyes again. A smile played about his lips.

'I don't deny that,' he said softly.

He wasn't sure what was happening to him, an unusual state of affairs for him. He was usually in total command when dallying with the ladies but there was something about this young woman that both intrigued and bewitched him. And there was something familiar about her.

He hadn't been aware of placing his left hand around her waist and drawing her close but he could feel the softness of her body against his and he lowered his head, gently touching her lips. He felt their warm, velvet touch quivering slightly, but unresisting, and he deepened the kiss.

By her tentative, yet willing, response, he realised that she was unused to kissing, a thought that made his heart unaccountably leap for joy. However, he didn't want to frighten her or make her despise his action and so he gently withdrew. He saw a look of wonderment in her eyes, a wonderment that matched his own.

'Yes, you are all woman,' he heard himself say softly.

A look of shame flittered across her face.

'I'm sorry! I didn't mean that as it sounded, nor did I mean to take advantage of your position here.'

He wasn't used to apologising for kissing a young lady and he feared he was doing it badly. He saw her bite her lip uncertainly.

'Forgive me, Miss Faversham. I

meant no offence.'

Eleanor bowed her head slightly.

'I am not offended, sir.'

She paused and then grinned mischievously.

'Though maybe I should be! I was as willing as you were. It was nothing, nothing to take exception to. That is . . . '

Her voice faltered, as if uncertain how to proceed. She seemed relieved when Lord Stansfield took a small step back.

'As I was saying, we have a problem,' he said, as if the interruption hadn't occurred. 'We have to return to France for the rest of our cargo.

'France?'

'Yes. That is where we collect, but the two men who were in the rowing boat cannot return there. We need to land them and Master Varney. There are many safe places. However, it might be dangerous. We have no way of knowing which places are being watched, and you aren't used to rough travelling. The alternative is that you come with me.'

Eleanor gasped.

'Come with you? But, I have no papers. How will I be allowed in?'

Lord Stansfield grinned.

'When you sail with me you do not need papers.'

'No, of course not. How silly of me. But, is this not dangerous also?'

Lord Stansfield's face sobered.

'Yes,' he agreed quietly. 'It has danger but you do not have to leave the ship. However, it will be of benefit to have you aboard if our mission ends favourably.'

'Are your illegal dealings really worth all this?' Eleanor asked, her voice cold again. 'Men could have lost their lives this night. And for what? Rich men's indulgences and the playing of childish games.'

'We are playing no games! Our aim is to save lives, not lose them!'

Eleanor didn't have the chance to say what she thought, as a loud cry rent the air. Eleanor left Lord Stansfield's side and ran across the deck to where the group of sailors was gathered around the man who had received one of the excisemen's bullets. The injured man let out a cry, as a seaman dug out the bullet from his arm and then poured some brandy from a flask on to the wound.

'Is he qualified to do that?' Eleanor asked, as she watched.

'He's done it before, if that's what you mean,' Lord Stansfield murmured.

'Well, I sincerely hope that I don't end up under his knife! That man's arm needs a dressing on it.'

The self-appointed surgeon tore a strip off the sailor's torn sleeve.

'Not that! It isn't clean! Wait!'

She turned her back on the group and lifted up the hem of her skirt.

'Give me your knife!' she bade the nearest seaman.

Grinning broadly, the seaman complied. Ignoring the broad grins and ribald comments, Eleanor briskly slashed at her cotton petticoat and tore off a jagged length from around the hem.

'Right! That should do. Allow me!'

She dropped to her knees by the injured man's side, and deftly began to bind the strip of fabric around the bleeding wound. When it was wrapped round a number of times, she slashed the remaining length down the middle and took the two lengths in opposite directions around the dressing, ending by tying two knots to secure it in place.

Lord Stansfield put a hand under her elbow and raised her to her feet. The admiration in his eyes was genuine.

'You may release me, my lord. I feel quite steady.'

'Good. You did well, there. It will stand you in good stead with the men.'

'What do you mean?'

'An old seaman's tradition is to look with some foreboding on the presence of a woman on board. It's not as strong as it was, but it still persists in some parts. Your lack of squeamishness has probably impressed them, as it did me! It bodes fair for your rôle in our next move.'

‘Which will be?’

‘After we have set down Master Varney and our two guests, we will make for the open sea. It is too late to hope to reach France on this evening’s tide, so we must await the next one.’

‘What is special about the evening tide?’

‘We need the maximum amount of water to reach our picking-up point safely and the cover of darkness makes us less likely to be seen. The tides are running high at the moment and are at their highest at just after midnight for the next two nights. The moon presents a bit of a problem as it gives us no cover but, on the positive side, we need no lanterns to see by, and it will reveal our attackers, should anyone be lying in wait for us. Hopefully, they will think us gone for the time being and will be looking elsewhere.’

Eleanor forbore to ask for more details, not wanting to be drawn into argument concerning his illicit travel and trade again.

'What d'you want me to do, mister?' Bertie asked suddenly.

Lord Stansfield weighed him up.

'You may land with Master Varney, if you wish, though it may be better if they have no encumbrances. Have you got your sea-legs, lad?'

'I have that! It's great, this is! Can I stay with you, then?'

'If you wish, but you must obey my orders strictly. I'll have no wilful behaviour or any tricks. As for you, Miss Faversham, I think it as well if you go down below out of the cold night air.'

'Might I not wait until after Master Varney and the two foreign men are put ashore, as long as I won't be in your way, that is?'

She was gratified to find an answering smile light up his face.

'It is lovely tonight, isn't it?' he answered. 'I take it that this is your first sea voyage, Miss Faversham.'

'It is indeed, and I'm loving every minute of it, apart from the danger, of course,' she added as an afterthought.

'Of course,' he echoed, feeling as if he were swimming in the depths of her sparkling eyes. 'Very well, but remain totally silent once we are near the shore. Sounds carry far over water and we mustn't alert any coastguards!'

It was a magical night, and so easy to forget that an all-too-real danger lurked close at hand. At a given signal, Lord Stansfield changed abruptly from a courtly, debonair lord of the realm to decisive leader, giving orders in a quiet, firm voice that defied argument.

Whilst the ship rode at anchor, two sailors, Master Varney and the two Frenchmen slipped silently over the side and huddled low in the rowing boat. They pulled almost silently towards the towering cliffs and seemed to be swallowed by the dark shadows. Those waiting on the ship held their breath, straining their ears for any sound that might announce that they had been apprehended. No sound came and, eventually, they could see the small boat slowly returning with Master Varney as its only occupant.

Once it had been tied securely to the stern of the schooner, they weighed anchor. The ship rose on its keel and sliced through the waves. Dawn was streaking the eastern sky. It was breathtakingly beautiful and it was with some reluctance that Eleanor went below to a small, but extremely neat cabin. The bunk was quite long and she wondered if she were in Lord Stansfield's bed. The thought didn't make falling asleep easy but, at some point, when the sun was rising high in the sky, her eyes closed and she drifted into a dreamless sleep.

7

Eleanor slept peacefully through the greater part of the day, the gentle rocking motion of the sea lulling her slumbers. When she finally emerged on deck, it was to a glorious, autumn day.

'Where's Lord Stansfield?' she inquired of the captain.

'Resting. We have a busy night in front of us.'

'Ah, yes! More cargo! Tell me, Captain Denbigh, don't you think he should be resting on his laurels, hanging up his anchor, or whatever it is that smugglers do when they retire?'

'Oh, he's not a . . . '

' . . . about to retire,' Lord Stansfield's voice murmured in her ear. 'There's life in the old dog yet, you know!'

Eleanor pursed her lips and drew herself up tall.

'Well, it's time you stopped playing games and took your responsible place in Society. I just don't want to hear of you getting hurt, and all for a few bottles of brandy or whatever it is you are smuggling.'

Lord Stansfield's eyes softened as he looked down at her.

'I appreciate your concern, but I must do what I must do.'

He took hold of her hand.

'Would you really be unhappy if I were to be hurt?'

'I . . . yes, I would.'

'Then I shall do my utmost to avoid getting into any difficulties. At the end of this evening's work, I will abide by your decision as to whether or not I continue, or hang up my anchor as you put it. What do you say?'

Eleanor was surprised that he was willing to capitulate so readily. Her heart leaped. Was he not indifferent to her feelings then?

'You do me a great honour, my lord.'

Lord Stansfield's eyes seemed to

convey a depth of feeling that made Eleanor's heart race. As he moved over to Captain Denbigh in order to discuss their evening plans, Eleanor felt both bereft and relieved. Her emotions were tumbling over each other. How could he be interested in her? He was a member of the nobility and rich, she supposed, whereas she was a penniless nobody, an accused thief, moreover, and an impersonator!

Convinced that she was over-reacting to Lord Stansfield's attention to her, Eleanor felt her elation drain away. She was unused to courtly ways and the interaction between Lord Stansfield and the woman named as Lavinia on the balcony at the Assembly Rooms showed that they paid exaggerated compliments to each other. He was merely being gallant and she must regard his words as such.

With nightfall came longed-for clouds. The schooner sailed as near to the vicinity of land as they dared and dropped anchor.

At the very moment that Lord Stansfield and one of the crew were about to climb over the side into the rowing boat, a small sloop was spotted heading their way. Even as they watched, a puff of smoke indicated that they were being fired upon, though the shot fell far short of them.

A mild oath fell from Lord Stansfield's lips.

'Captain Denbigh! A change of plan, I think. Miss Faversham, will you be so good as to accompany me on this inshore trip? I have no wish to leave you on board whilst we are being fired upon.'

'We'll lead 'em a dance, Jem!' Captain Denbigh promised.

'We'll meet at point B. Good luck!' Lord Stansfield called.

With a pounding heart, Eleanor followed him down the rope ladder into the small craft. They cast off immediately, Lord Stansfield and the sailor pulling hard on the oars, taking the boat into a narrow creek with high rocks on either side. The waterway grew more and more narrow, until the two oarsmen slipped their oars and used their hands against the rocks to propel the boat forward. At last, Lord Stansfield leaped ashore, hauling on the rope fixed to the prow and holding it steady.

He held out his other hand for Eleanor to grasp and she stepped carefully on to the rock at his side. She felt warmed by his closeness, but Lord Stansfield had already let go of her hand and was tying the rope around a jagged rock. Eleanor felt hampered by her skirts as they scrambled over the rocks. Lord Stansfield's hand was ever ready to assist her over the more difficult parts and she was relieved when they reached the base of the cliffs.

'Check if they're in the cave, Sam!' he murmured quietly.

Sam was soon back.

'Cave empty,' he mouthed briefly.

'Right, we go up the cliff to the inn. Move carefully. Silence is essential.'

It was easier than the scramble over

the rocks but Eleanor was glad when they reached the top. It felt very exposed up there but the terrain soon dropped into a series of hollows and rocky outcrops that gave some shelter.

The banging of a door alerted her to the near proximity of a building but, the moment they were engulfed in its shadows, they became aware of sounds of movements and foreign voices giving orders. Sounds of feet ringing on the cobbles and the neighing of horses reached them.

They pressed themselves against the walls of an outbuilding. Lord Stansfield put out a hand to halt their progress.

'French guards!' he mouthed quietly. 'They're searching the buildings.'

They froze against the wall, Eleanor's heart pounding with fear. What would happen if they were caught? England wasn't at war with France at the moment but that their business was suspect would be all too obvious! A few shouts, banging of doors and then the sound of heavy footsteps on the cobbled yard faded slightly. Lord Stansfield crept forward to the end of the wall and peered cautiously round the side. His dark figure disappeared.

His silent figure was soon back at their side.

'They've found nothing. They're going back into the inn. You two slip into this building. I'm going to see if I can get into the inn without being seen.'

Sam hustled her into the building, which was a stable. A number of horses were snorting restlessly, and a cart stood to one side, one wooden side let down, showing it to be empty apart from some sacking.

'Keep in the shadows, miss, just in case!' Sam warned.

There were more shouts, the ringing sound of hooves and of men running. Not being able to understand the shouts didn't help to calm them. They just had to keep still and wait. Suddenly, the door swung open.

Eleanor gasped and Sam clapped a

hand unceremoniously over her mouth, pulling her back towards him. She felt him relax.

'It's Jem,' he murmured quietly. 'Sorry, miss!'

He let go of her and moved forward towards the shadowy figure. Then Eleanor realised there was more than one figure. There was another man and a small figure clinging to him. Lord Stansfield uttered a few foreign words and the small figure was thrust towards Eleanor.

'Help her up on to the cart!' Lord Stansfield ordered quietly. 'Then get up yourself. Sam, fasten the sides up and then you, too, get on board.'

As he spoke, he and the other man were backing one of the horses between the shafts of the cart. Then they were doing something around the horse's feet.

'We're muffling the hooves,' Lord Stansfield explained.

The child was sobbing and Eleanor hugged her close, wondering who she was and why she was here. The doors of the stable were opened wide and the two men led the horse and cart into the yard. Both men then climbed up on to the driving seat. With a gentle flick on the reins, the horse was urged into motion. Rain was falling now. Eleanor shivered and drew the child close to her. The girl had stopped crying.

'It's all right!' Eleanor consoled her.

The girl's body was convulsed with tremors. Who was she? And what about the contraband they should have collected? Had the journey been in vain? Maybe they were now on their way to pick it up. Sam tossed the sacking over them and Eleanor murmured her thanks.

'Somebody saw our arrival and alerted the guards,' Lord Stansfield spoke over his shoulder. 'They have gone to the cliffs to search for us, which gives us time to make our departure another way. Hold steady!'

They had left the confines of the yard and, in response to the given command, the horse increased its pace.

'Where are we going, Sam?'

'Back to rejoin the Mary Jane. There's a larger creek a few miles south. If we make good time, we should still catch the ebb tide. With any luck the Mary Jane will be waiting for us.'

Within the half-hour, he announced that he could see the ship down below. The cart halted and Lord Stansfield leaped down.

'Come on! We've no time to lose.'

He took the girl from Eleanor's arms. Sam assisted Eleanor down and then refastened the wooden side. The driver had lit a lantern and was shining its light towards the ship. A similar gleam from the ship gave answer. Lord Stansfield extinguished the light and handed back the lantern to the driver.

'Au revoir, Anton! A bientôt!'

The cart rumbled away and the four of them made their way swiftly to the cliff top. A steep path led downwards. Lord Stansfield carried the girl on his shoulders. Sam almost leaped down the path ahead of him and Eleanor stepped and slithered as best she could. A few shouts from the cliff top drew their eyes anxiously upwards and spurred their steps forward. A low mist hung over the water. If they could only get to that, they would be safe!

A shout from just below them hastened their steps in the right direction as they reached the shore. Lord Stansfield leaped from rock to rock, his burden seeming to be no hindrance. Having deposited her into the boat, he returned to take Eleanor's hand over the last few steps. They paid no heed to the shouts behind them, nor of the pistol shots that rang out.

'Get down in the boat!' Lord Stansfield commanded them, as he and the other sailors took the oars.

It was a larger boat than the one they had abandoned and now had four oarsmen to pull it beyond the pistol range. To Eleanor's great relief, they were soon swallowed by the mist. Before long, the dark shape of the schooner towered over them. Eager hands helped them on board and, without more ado, the ship sprang into motion. Eleanor clung to the rail.

'Well done, you darling girl!'

Lord Stansfield's arm had slipped around her waist. Eleanor turned to face him.

'I did nothing spectacular,' she felt obliged to apologise.

His other arm was holding the child close to him.

'You kept your head and responded without question,' he complimented. 'I'm only too sorry I felt compelled to take you with me, but I feared for the ship's safety, and yours,' he added softly.

'And I for you,' she admitted quietly, risking a glance at his face.

He was looking adoringly at her. His glance confused her.

'We must see to the child,' she said, to cover her confusion. 'She's cold and terrified. Shall I take her below?'

Lord Stansfield swept the girl into his arms.

'Will you mind sharing your cabin with her? She's called Lucille, by the way. I owe you an explanation about tonight's deeds, but will you let it wait until morning? Right now, you both need warmth and comfort.'

Eleanor nodded her agreement. She, too, owed him some explanations, but she still wasn't sure she would be able to face making them.

'Don't worry that she can't understand you,' Lord Stansfield added. 'The tone of your voice will comfort her. Poor child! She has lost all of her family.'

8

Eleanor found a tub of warm water awaiting them in the cabin below and after being sponged with the warm water and rubbed down briskly, Lucille crouched in the corner of the cabin whilst Eleanor stripped herself of her wet clothing and wrapped herself up in one of the voluminous towels Lord Stansfield had provided.

Lord Stansfield brought two bowls of hot broth for them. Eleanor had to spoon-feed Lucille, as the child was shaking too much to hold the spoon without spilling the broth. She tried to make it into a game but knew that Lucille couldn't understand anything she said to her. Likewise, Eleanor couldn't understand the few words that Lucille cried out in her distress, except maman and papa. All she could do was hug her close and rock her in her arms,

They spent the night curled together in the narrow bunk.

The poor child! Eleanor thought of the tales that she had heard, tales that told of the deeds of terror across the Channel. It came as no surprise, therefore, when Lord Stansfield told her that this was the case, when he brought back their dried clothing.

He told her about the sudden arrest and execution of Lucille's parents, part of the Reign of Terror that was sweeping through France; of Lucille's rescue by a faithful servant and about his involvement with a group of Englishmen who had made a pact to rescue as many such victims as they could, legally or illegally, and how Lucille's rescuers hadn't been able to get her to the departure point on time.

Eleanor found herself blushing in embarrassment.

'I thought you were a smuggler! How foolish you must have thought me.'

Lord Stansfield's eyes twinkled with amusement.

'I did consider putting a patch over one eye to live up to the part you claimed for me, but the danger was far too real for such levity.'

'You risked your life to save Lucille, and your men did, as well. And Adèle? You rescued her, too, didn't you? And others?'

It was Lord Stansfield's turn to be embarrassed. He shrugged carelessly.

'My men take greater risks than I, especially those who live in France.'

'What will happen to Lucille now?'

She hugged the child by her side, withdrawn and silent.

'That's something we need to think about carefully, but not now. I have things to do. Can you manage to dress yourselves?'

Eleanor laughed out loud.

'You forget, my lord, I have never had a servant in my life. In fact, the highest I can hope for is to become one myself.'

Lord Stansfield's face sobered.

'You, a servant? Never!'

Eleanor felt stricken. He had changed

his mind, then. He now considered her unsuitable to become Lucille's maid. Was it because the child was so young? Did he think her unsuitable to care for a child, or had she disappointed him in some way?

He appeared not to notice her shock at his words. After reminding her to go up on deck after they were dressed and had breakfasted, he bowed and left them. Eleanor felt the disappointment keenly. She had felt that her immediate future was secure but, now, a bleak future stretched ahead of her once again. Quelling her fears for the sake of the child, she dressed them both and, after breakfasting on fruit, she took Lucille up on deck. The child clung tenaciously to her hand. Eleanor was surprised to find that they were in sight of land.

'Is that England?' she asked a passing seaman.

'Aye, miss.'

So, they were almost home, her adventure over! Lord Stansfield stood at the helm with Captain Denbigh. He hailed their appearance.

'Miss Faversham! We are about to land. Have you got everything you came with?'

Eleanor, determined to hide her apprehension about her future, smiled.

'I have, and more besides!' she answered, looking down at Lucille.

Bertie was nearby, busy helping a sailor.

'I'm staying here, Miss Ella, as a deckhand!' he said happily. 'You brought me good luck!'

'I'm glad of that!'

But what about herself? She was too proud to beg assistance.

Lucille and Eleanor were helped over the side into the rowing boat. Even though Lord Stansfield had expressed his lack of need of her, she was relieved that he was to accompany them on the last stage of their journey.

'I'm afraid that, since we left the country illegally, we must re-enter the same way,' he said wryly, as he handed her to the seat in the stern. 'Once safely ashore, we will return to Dover by hired coach.'

She felt her spirit sinking lower. They would be parting soon and she found it difficult to contemplate the fact.

Fortune was now smiling upon them and they landed without mishap. Lord Stansfield had obviously been here before and he led the way confidently from the quiet cove to a small inn. From there, they went by an ancient carriage to a posting house near Folkestone. There were no vehicles for hire and Eleanor found herself to be relieved to have to travel to Dover by the Royal Mail coach. She needed time to nurse her bruised heart and knew she would have found a privately-hired carriage far too intimate. Lord Stansfield advised Eleanor not to divulge anything of their recent few days.

'People may assume we are a family. Let the assumption stand. A careless word could land us in trouble with the authorities.'

He crouched down in front of Lucille and spoke some words Eleanor didn't understand.

'I have told her not to speak at all, as it would draw unwelcome attention to us,' he explained as he straightened. 'If people ask, tell them she doesn't travel well, that it makes her nauseous. How are you? Are you up to this?'

Eleanor composed her thoughts and managed a wan smile.

'Yes, of course.'

It wouldn't be difficult to pretend they were a family. The difficult part would be to leave it all behind.

Lucille clung to her hand throughout the journey, her face pale and apprehensive. Her recent experiences had taught her to trust no-one. Eleanor was touched to realise that that didn't include her, but how would Lucille fare when she left them? It would be like another betrayal.

Mistress Varney gave them a warm welcome when they arrived at the inn. The two Frenchmen had already departed to the next refuge along Lord Stansfield's devised route for their safety.

'The poor little mite,' Mrs Varney sympathised.

She led the way once more to the room where she kept the assortment of clothing and they soon had a number of suitable outfits for Lucille to wear until she was established in some benefactor's care. Eleanor chattered about the clothes as she washed Lucille's hair and then bathed her and was gratified to receive some glimmers of smiles.

She had already established their names by the simple expediency of saying, 'You, Lucille. Me, Eleanor,' hoping that the use of her Christian name would be acceptable to Lord Stansfield, and she named each article of clothing as she dressed the girl in a mid-blue, wide-skirted gown of softest merino wool. She was delighted when Lucille echoed the words, then nonplussed when Lucille followed it up with a strange word. Then she realised that Lucille was giving her the French words!

'Good!' she applauded. 'I teach you English. You teach me French!'

She was rewarded with a huge smile, which transformed Lucille's face. Eleanor hugged her. If only she might stay with Lucille, she was sure she would be able to help her to settle in her new country. She would persuade Lord Stansfield somehow that she was a suitable person to care for Lucille.

She dressed herself in a simple day-gown of russet serge. Her fingers brushed her mother's locket and, for a moment, she held it tightly in her hand, suddenly feeling as lacking in family as Lucille.

'Come, Lucille, let's find Lord Stansfield.'

He, too, had changed his clothes and looked relaxed and debonair. He was reading the early-morning news sheet but rose to his feet immediately as they entered the room. His face froze for a moment and Eleanor wondered what she had done wrong. Did the gown not look right on her? Or had he changed his mind about giving her the gowns? She felt like fleeing back to her room, but Lucille moved forward, pulling Eleanor with her.

Lord Stansfield swept his body into an elaborate bow.

'Ladies!'

Lucille, young as she was, showed her breeding and dropped into a formal curtsey, murmuring, 'Monsieur,' to which Lord Stansfield responded again. Eleanor stood like a statue, watching the display of courtly behaviour, feeling very much on the outside. No wonder Lord Stansfield thought her unfit to take any part in Lucille's upbringing! She felt gauche and untutored.

Lord Stansfield spoke some words in French. A glimmer of interest sparked on Lucille's face and she stepped forward, holding out her hands expectantly. Lord Stansfield reached down at the side of his vacated chair and picked up something he had placed there previously. It was a doll. Smiling, he held it out to her and she took it out of his hands, instantly clutching it to her.

'Merci bien, monsieur!'

She sank on to the rug in front of the log fire, smoothing her fingers over the doll, her face showing her delight. Eleanor's face softened as she watched her. Lord Stansfield indicated that she sit and she did so, thankful that his attention was on Lucille. Or was it?

'You are quiet,' Lord Stansfield observed, as he sat beside her.

Eleanor's head shot up, meeting his gaze.

'Yes. I was enjoying watching Lucille play with the doll. It was very kind of you to think of it. She is a lovely child. I tremble to think what might have become of her if you hadn't risked your life to save her.'

He reached across and took hold of her hand.

'Do I now have your blessing on my maritime activities?'

His eyes were twinkling, as he

awaited her reaction. Eleanor looked down, her cheeks burning. She made herself meet his gaze.

'Yes, you do, though I fear for your safety. Oh, dear, I mean, I would fear, if I was to know about it, but I don't expect I shall. So . . . '

Embarrassed by her confused words, she broke off abruptly.

'My dear Eleanor . . . I may call you by your Christian name, may I?'

'Yes, if you wish.'

'Dear Eleanor, I didn't mean to speak of this quite so soon. I don't wish to frighten you but . . . '

'Oh!' Eleanor's heart plummeted. 'You wish me to go?'

'Go? No! I want you to stay!'

'Stay where? Here?'

'No! With me!'

Eleanor's fingers clutched at her locket nervously.

'With you?'

'Not yet! It wouldn't be at all proper, though we have already spent two nights unchaperoned, haven't we? Dammit! You'll have to marry me!'

His face was aglow, his eyes dancing with merriment.

Eleanor felt the blood drain from her face in genuine shock.

'I can't marry you!'

Lord Stansfield looked shocked now.

'Why not? But you must!'

'But, your reputation? You would be ruined if you were to marry me.'

His eyes twinkled.

'But what about your reputation if I don't?'

'Mine? I haven't got a reputation. At least, none that I care to keep!'

A thief! That was her reputation. She certainly mustn't even consider marrying Lord Stansfield.

'You must not tease me like this, my lord!'

Lord Stansfield stroked his thumb across the knuckles of her hand.

'My darling girl, I am not teasing you. We have defied convention in the past two days, and are doing so even now. Dear Eleanor, you must be aware that I have, shall we say, fond feelings for you?'

'Have you? Oh, dear! I mean . . . '

'I know we haven't known each other for more than a couple of days, but I have never felt like this about anyone in my whole life. Never dreamed I ever would. And I would very much like your permission to pay court to you.'

'Pay court? You mean . . . '

Her mind was racing round in circles. He loved her! He wanted to marry her! He didn't want her to go!

'I want to come a-courting, dear girl!'

'Oh, but are you sure?'

'Never been more so!'

'But I'm penniless. I'm no match for you.'

She must put him off the idea. He wouldn't love her if he really knew her.

'Everyone will think you have chosen beneath you!'

'My darling, it's a daunting thought, but I'm so rich, no-one will say a word against us.'

'But they will think it!'

She disengaged her hand from his and rose to her feet. She swallowed hard, knowing she was about to break her heart with her words.

'I am a nobody, my lord. No-one will think any worse of you, or me, because of our two days of enforced companionship. I shall never speak of it, so no-one who matters will know. You are under no sort of obligation.'

Lord Stansfield had risen and was now standing in front of her. He tried to take hold of her hand again but she fended him away, her left hand now clutching her locket, drawing strength from the tenuous link with her mother.

'Let me continue. I thank you for the honour you intend but you will quickly realise that it really would not do. Yes, you would!'

She stepped back again as he moved towards her.

'There is one thing I would beg of you. Would it be possible for you to . . . '

Her voice was shaking, but she must continue.

‘I know you said that I could not be Lucille’s maid, that I am unsuitable in some way, but I beg you to reconsider and recommend me as maid for Lucille to whoever you choose to become her guardian.’

The last few words hurtled from her lips, anxious for the humiliation of pleading for a job to be over. Lord Stansfield placed his hands upon her shoulders and looked down into her eyes.

‘You have not changed my mind,’ he said softly, ‘but I will leave it for now. I have spoken too hastily and alarmed you. I did not intend so.’

His eyes focussed suddenly on her locket. He looked perplexed.

‘Is this yours? I mean, has it always been yours, or have you only recently acquired it?’

‘Of course, it’s mine! My mother gave it to me. It’s all I have left of her. And, before you ask, no, she didn’t steal it. No matter what my uncle says, she wasn’t a thief, and neither am I.’

A slight change came over his

expression. His eyes narrowed and there was a strange look in them. Eleanor couldn't quite fathom his expression. His eyes held a mixture of tenderness, wonder and — triumph? For what reason would he look triumphant? What was he thinking?

He took the locket from her shaking fingers and studied its engraving.

'May I see it more closely?'

'Yes, but why?'

Her fingers fumbled at the clasp of the chain behind her neck. Lord Stansfield stepped behind her and Eleanor's trembling hands lifted her hair out of the way, allowing him to undo the clasp.

'Does it open?' he asked.

Eleanor turned round to face him.

'It should, but it has always been stuck. My mother said her likeness is inside it, but I have never wanted to risk damaging it beyond repair. So, I have never seen it. It is mine, though. I haven't stolen it. I haven't stolen anything.'

Lord Stansfield's glance moved from her eyes to the locket and back again. His next words shattered the cocoon of warmth his expressions of love had wrapped around her.

'I would beg to differ, my dear Eleanor. There is something you have stolen.'

9

Eleanor felt the shock of his words. Her mind, her whole body froze into immobility. What did he mean?

Lord Stansfield bowed low over Eleanor's hand. It was a formal bow and his face, when he rose, was now inscrutable.

'I have a journey to make, Miss Faversham. I must ask you to remain here until I return. Whilst I am away, I will arrange for your locket to be opened and repaired. I may be away two days but I will leave instructions with Mistress Varney for your welfare.'

He dropped on to his knees at the side of Lucille and spoke rapidly some words in French. Lucille listened gravely and nodded. She then looked at Eleanor and nodded again. With a farewell, flamboyant bow, Lord Stansfield then strode from the room.

Eleanor watched him go with pain in her heart. Why did he think her a thief? Surely he knew that it wasn't so. She couldn't understand his contradictory behaviour. One minute he was asking her to marry him, and the next saying she was a thief. It didn't make sense.

The two days passed slowly. She spent the time getting to know Lucille better and they taught each other a number of elementary words in each other's language. They walked along the cliff tops, scrambled down the cliff path and played on the shingle. They joined Mistress Varney in the kitchen, appreciating her hot, buttered scones and her freshly-made bread with lovely butter and jam spread over.

It was on the third day when the rumble of carriage wheels alerted them to Lord Stansfield's return. When they peeped through the window, both of them were amazed to see not one carriage but two! Eleanor drew back from the mullioned windows, not wanting her curiosity to be noticed.

Lucille had no such scruples. She pressed her nose to the glass, exclaiming excitedly in her own language. Eleanor's heart sank when she saw two young women descend from the second carriage. She could tell by their clothes that they were of the serving class. Lord Stansfield must be intending to dispense with her services immediately. What would she do? Where could she go?

Her heart thumped painfully as Lord Stansfield's footsteps approached. How could she face him? Fortunately, Lucille drew his attention. She ran across to him, her words of welcome tumbling from her lips, holding her doll for him to greet. He laughed at her delight in seeing him and held out his hand towards Eleanor, to draw her into the welcome, but Eleanor held back. This was going to be hard enough to cope with. She needed to remain cool and detached, or, at least, to pretend to be so.

Lord Stansfield spoke some words to

Lucille. The girl looked at him doubtfully but, in response to some more words, she went towards the door, where she paused to wave a brief farewell to Eleanor. Eleanor felt a sob rushing to her throat. Was this to be their goodbye?

'My lord, you treat me too harshly. Am I not even to be allowed to say farewell to Lucille? You are too cruel.'

She felt unwanted tears pricking at her eyes and tried to brush past Lord Stansfield, her head down, hoping to make her escape to the privacy of her room. Lord Stansfield grasped her arm, restraining her progress.

'Don't run away, Eleanor. I want to explain myself.'

'I think your actions speak for you, my lord!' Eleanor choked out. 'Pray, let me pass. You will be free of my presence as soon as I gather my things.'

She realised that she had nothing to gather. All she owned was upon her person and this unfeeling, insufferable, hard-hearted man had given her even those!

'Eleanor, my darling girl, I don't wish to be free of your presence. I want to have and to hold you until death do us part.'

His eyes smiled down at her, sending warm hope into her heart.

'But that's part of the wedding ceremony!'

'I know! I did ask you to marry me, remember?'

'Yes, but you said . . . '

She could hardly frame the words in her mind, let alone with her lips.

'You said that you think me a thief.'

'You have stolen my heart, Eleanor! Can I hope that you will reconsider and give me yours?'

He stroked his fingers down the side of her face, teasing a golden strand of hair into corkscrew spirals around one of his fingers.

Eleanor caught her breath.

'But you know it is not wise. I thought you understood, that you agreed it would be foolish. Don't tease me thus, my lord. It is difficult enough for me to refuse your kind offer.'

'There is nothing kind about my offer. I love you desperately and will not be responsible for my actions if you persist in refusing me. I am being insufferably selfish in insisting on having my way in this matter but I warn you, I will not be denied.'

Eleanor thought she must be dreaming or suffering a delusion.

'But, you must! I cannot allow you to throw yourself away on me, a penniless nobody!'

She must not allow him to sway her. Her breath caught as she realised that he was lowering his head to hers and his lips were about to meet hers. Oh, his kiss was wonderful! If this were all she ever had of him, she would still remember it until the day she died.

'You were saying?'

'Was I? Oh, yes.'

Her brain was reeling. What had she been saying? That he mustn't marry her? Mustn't kiss her?

'Oh, dear!'

'You are weakening!' he teased.

'Yes, my lord, but have you considered . . .'

'I haven't considered anything beyond that I love you and am determined to have you. And will you try to call me Jeremy? It is my given name.'

'Yes, I know.'

'Then try it! Come on. It is quite easy!'

'Yes . . . Jeremy.'

'There! We are as good as engaged already!'

He laughed at her scandalised expression.

'Dearest Eleanor, you are adorable! I swear we shall not have a dull marriage.'

Eleanor was still bemused. He loved her! He truly did! His face sobered.

'But we need to talk, my dear. I must admit to have been teasing you somewhat shamefully.'

A tremor of shock sped through her.

'Teasing me?'

Lord Stansfield swept her into his arms again.

'Not about loving you. Come and sit down and let me explain.'

He led her to the two-seater settle by the fireside. She sank upon it, gratefully, followed by his lordship. He was still holding her hand as he reached into his pocket, withdrawing a small packet. When he opened the packet, Eleanor saw her locket resting in his hand.

'Oh, my locket!' she cried. 'You have brought it back. Did you manage to get it opened?'

'I did.'

He held the locket in his fingers, smoothing his thumb over the engraved pattern on the front.

'I recognised your locket when I saw it three days ago. Yes, you may well blush, you minx! I saw it first upon a delightful young lady pretending to be a French émigrée in the Assembly Ballroom, though I knew her to be no more French than I am! No, let me finish,' he interrupted as she tried to explain.

'That young lady bewitched me and I was determined to discover who she was, since she fled from the ball before I could learn her real name!'

Eleanor's red cheeks burned with embarrassment.

'So, early the next day, I began to make some enquiries. However, before I could follow them up, I was summoned upon our little adventure. I suspected that this crest on your locket belongs to the Wooding family, who reside in Sussex, which is where I have been these past days. I had a very interesting talk with Sir Lawrence Wooding. He showed me a portrait of his daughter, who bore a surprising resemblance to you. When I showed him this locket, he seized it from my hand, almost overcome with emotion. He knew it to have belonged to his daughter.'

Eleanor gasped.

'His daughter? You mean my mother? Sir Lawrence?'

'Sir Lawrence Wooding, a gentleman

of the first rank. He was a friend of my father's and has remained within our family circle since my father's death.'

'And he is my grandfather?'

'I believe so, and so does he. Look!'

Eleanor held her breath as he opened the locket and held it out towards her. She took it from him and gazed at the small likeness of a young woman whose features were those in her memories of her mother.

'My mamma,' she breathed softly.

'Yes, your mother was undoubtedly Sir Lawrence's younger daughter. She fell in love with a shoemaker's son and, when the match was forbidden, she ran away. She was never seen again, though searches were made.'

Eleanor found it difficult to breathe.

'She always told me she was a lady. My uncle called her a liar and a thief, but I knew she wasn't!'

'No indeed! A little naïve and impetuous, perhaps, but certainly no thief. As for you, my love, your arguments against our marriage are swept away. On my part, this knowledge makes no difference. I would have won your heart anyway, as you have won mine. In fact, I do believe I already have.'

He raised her hand to his lips and kissed each finger in turn, watching as she blushed most prettily, her golden eyelashes fluttering on her cheeks.

'So, I have a family after all.'

'Indeed you do! You have lots of aunts and uncles, cousins, and a grandfather aching to dote upon you. I am instructed to bear you hence with the utmost speed. Your grandfather has sent two maids to accompany you, and has given me permission to court you properly, as Society demands!'

'Oh!'

It was a deep sigh of happiness, straight from her heart. Then, a sudden alarm stilled her.

'But what of Lucille? I had hoped you might allow me . . . well, it sounds silly now, but I can't bear to think of losing her.'

'Ah, well, my love, I thought as much. See how I already leap to obey your slightest wish?'

He put a finger under her chin and tilted up her face to kiss her lightly.

'And so, I had a word with your grandfather and, between us, we came up with the idea that your grandfather will accept guardianship of her, until we are married, and then we . . . '

'Oh, Jeremy! You truly are the most wonderful man I have ever met!'

'I know,' he agreed modestly, his eyes sparkling. 'And you are the most delightful woman I have ever met. I think, between us, we will make the most remarkable of marriages, don't you?'

Eleanor sighed happily.

'Oh, yes!'

Other titles in the
Linford Romance Library:

TO BE WITH YOU

Audrey Weigh

Heather, the proud owner of a small bus line, loves the countryside in her corner of Tasmania. Her life begins to change when two new men move into the area. Colin's charm overcomes her first resistance, while Grant also proves a warmer person than expected. But Colin is jealous when Grant gains special attention. The final test comes with the prospect of living in Hobart. Could Heather bear to leave her home and her business to be with the man she loves?

PERILOUS JOURNEY

Caroline Joyce

After the execution of Charles I, Louisa's Royalist father considers it too dangerous for her to stay in England and arranges for her to go to the Isle of Man with Armand de la Tremouille, the nephew of the island's Royalist Governor. Their ship is boarded by Parliamentarians who plan to sail for Ireland, but a storm causes them to be ship-wrecked on the Calf of Man. Magnus Stapleton, the Parliamentarian chief, becomes infatuated with Louisa, but she has fallen in love with Armand.

THE GYPSY'S RETURN

Sara Judge

After the death of her cruel father, Amy Keene's stepbrother and step-sister treated her just as badly. Amy had two friends, old Dr. Hilland and the washerwoman, Rosalind, with her fatherless child Becky. When Rosalind falls ill, Amy is entrusted with a letter to be given to Becky on her marriage. When the letter's contents are discovered, it causes Amy both mental and physical suffering and sets the seal of fate upon Rosalind's gypsy friend, Elias Jones.

WEB OF DECEIT

Margaret McDonagh

A good-looking man turned up on Louise's doorstep one day, introducing himself as Daniel Kinsella, an Australian friend of her brother-in-law, Greg. He said he had come to stay whilst he did some research — apparently Greg had written to her about it. Louise's initial reaction was to turn him away, but he was very persuasive. However, she was to discover that Daniel had bluffed his way into her life, and soon she found herself caught up in his dangerous mission.